I0679031

The Drakonian Chronicles Book 1

B.D. Snowden

GEEKY GOTH PRESS

DEDICATION

This book is dedicated to the awesome readers who have become friends through the miracle of social media. I love you guys!

ACKNOWLEDGMENTS

The book wouldn't have been possible without the baristas at 8th Street Coffee House who kept me supplied with caffeine. Besides coffee a lot of work goes into creating a book for publication. I would like to give a shout out to my editor Nick and my amazing cover artist Lillian who worked their magic on my behalf.

1

"Alexis! You should wait for the rest of the team."

Alexis Carmichael pushed the dark curls that had escaped her clip out of her face. She was too close to stop now. They had just breached the outer wall and she knew from the ground radar that a vast chamber that no human had entered for hundreds if not thousands of years was literally inches away from her. Her excitement couldn't be contained, and she would be damned if she let her assistant slow her down.

"I'm almost there, Charlie. I'm not going to fucking let Dr. Monroe get a look at this before I do."

It was well known amongst the members of the dig team that Dr. Carmichael and Dr. Monroe had a major rivalry going. What the team didn't know was that the two had been lovers when Alexis was still just a doctoral candidate. She had been attracted to the charismatic Dr. Monroe and naïve enough to take his flirtations seriously. It wasn't until later that Alexis had found out that the good doctor made a habit of banging any female he was an advisor for.

Once she had her degree conferred, she had made a point to avoid him whenever possible. This dig was her baby. It was her research that found the chamber beneath what everyone, even the locals, believed was just a hill in a meadow. So it really chapped Alexis's ass when the university had insisted that a more experienced archeologist be placed as co-director for this dig, otherwise their benefactor was going to pull the funding. Anyone else would have been fine, but they had to send Dr. Daniel Monroe, who was presently trying to get into the pants of nearly every female member of the team. *God, I should have cut his balls off years ago*, Alexis thought.

"Dr. Carmichael…" Oh no, Charlie was using her title. She absolutely hated making him feel uncomfortable, but this was her dig no matter what that pansy-ass Daniel Monroe thought.

"It will be fine, Charlie. I just want to look around. Nothing will be disturbed until properly documented and cataloged." Alexis' bright blue eyes looked over her shoulder. The sun was just coming out over the horizon. She had chosen to wake up early and work in the predawn hours because she knew that Daniel wouldn't be awake until the sun was well up. She needed this time of peace and quiet—without his casual touches. The man always seemed to be touching her. Alexis made a face.

Alexis removed the final stone. The opening was now wide enough for her to fit. She flicked on the headlamp on her helmet and slowly slithered her way through the opening. Charlie was relegated to standing watch outside of the chamber because of his large athletic frame.

A wide smile spread across her face as she surveyed the chamber and its contents. She had been certain that she had found a burial site of a high-value Celtic chieftain; but nothing prepared her for the wide range of artifacts that she was now faced

3

with. It was like she was in a European version of King Tut's tomb. This find was going to make her career.

Alexis did a silent little happy dance, which she stopped mid jiggle. She had forgotten, in her revelry, about Dr. Monroe. He was her own personal Rene Belloq. With a find this big it was a certainty that he would try to wrestle complete control and, along with it, the recognition. She could almost see him sneering at her and paraphrasing lines from *Indiana Jones*, "Dr. Carmichael, you see there is nothing you possess which I cannot take away."

"Fuck!" Alexis groused.

"What was that Dr. Carmichael?" Charlie's voice called from the entrance.

"Nothing…I'll be up in a few minutes. Go tell the rest of the team to get their butts into gear. We've got a lot of work to do."

Alexis could hear Charlie leaving to go get the rest of the team. She only had a few moments to get a private look. This find was like nothing else in this area. Other cairns, even the huge complexes, didn't have the riches that she was seeing here. Kings and great leaders had been buried with their arms and armor; a few had treasured household items or even animals. But this…. Everywhere Alexis turned…gold, gems, artwork. She walked deeper into the chamber. Her hands itched to touch the artifacts, to examine them more closely. She wouldn't, at least not until they were documented where they were found. The fact that a living person had not stepped foot into this space for over a thousand years made Alexis giddy.

Something on the far side of the chamber caught her eye. From a distance, it looked like a heavily carved floor-to-ceiling altar panel, but those weren't prevalent until the medieval period with the cathedral boom. As she was moving to investigate it further, she heard the clamoring of the rest of her dig team. Oh well, there was always time later to see what had caught her attention.

*****

Alexis ran her hand through her chin-length mahogany curls. The gesture was a sign of her frustration, but is also gave her a sexy, just-out-of-bed look. Six hours…the team had been tirelessly working for the last six hours and she had spent the last six hours fending off Monroe's advances. Good god, did the man actually do any work? She stalked off, hoping for a bit of a reprieve from his company.

5

Alexis wasn't a conventional beauty. She was short, barely over five feet tall. She had curves in all the right places, which kept her from seeming too petite and childlike. Her skin was peaches and cream, which contrasted greatly with the curly mass of dark hair that haloed her face. Her eyes were an amazing shade of sapphire blue framed by thick lashes. But the most amazing thing about her appearance was that she was oblivious to the effect she had on people. This was one of the reasons that every set of male eyes on the team followed her as she crossed the chamber.

Dr. Carmichael was all business. She wanted to examine the wall of relief carvings that had caught her attention when she first entered the chamber. She had always had an instinct for knowing when something was going to be important, and that sixth sense of hers was buzzing like a hive of bees at this point.

The closer Alexis got to the carving, the more her body hummed. She took out her soft-bristle brush and gently swept away centuries of dust and dirt. Underneath were the most exquisite carvings of stylized dragons that she had ever seen. She got down on her knees to follow one particular carving that seemed to draw her. The remaining flecks of paint that she so tenderly preserved showed that this dragon carving had at one time been red. Its shape was vaguely reminiscent of the Welsh *Y Ddraig Goch*, though it was positioned vertically, as if climbing down the wall. There was a similar dragon facing the opposite direction on the other side of the carving. If that dragon was colored white.... Alexis couldn't help the gleeful grin spreading across her face. Perhaps this may have been where that particular legend was born, since this chamber was estimated to predate any other references. Even without the impressive gold and artifacts, a find that pinpointed where a legend started would be a paper that could cement the name of Dr. Alexis Carmichael as one of the leading authorities on European history.

With her headlamp positioned to pick up the finer details, Alexis followed the body of the carving, starting at the head. As she moved up the length of the stone beast, Alexis noticed something strange. The claws of the dragon were carved in such a way that they seemed to be holding something.

Upon closer inspection Alexis realized that those claws weren't just carvings, but hinges. This wasn't just a magnificent piece of relief sculpture, but a door. Alexis examined the carving, and sure enough there was a barely discernible line right down the middle. She was standing in front of a massive carved double door.

Her mind started working at a hundred miles
an hour. It was possible that this door was placed
here because of its decorativeness, like a master
artwork. There was the chance that the door was
strictly symbolic or religious….a passageway into
the afterlife. But the last possibility was what
excited Alexis the most. It could just be a door that
leads to another chamber. If it did, it might be the
burial chamber, since the team had not found an
occupant for this tomb yet. *Oh, wouldn't it just chap
Monroe's ass if I found the burial chamber first,*
Alexis thought.

Trying not to draw any attention to herself,
Alexis went and fetched Charlie as well as one of the
interns who was cataloging items. Between the three
of them they measured, documented, and
photographed the doors.

The whole process was taking longer than
Alexis would like. So far her luck had held out and
Dr. Monroe had stayed away from her. Glancing
over her shoulder she saw him trying to smooze the
stunning blonde intern cataloging the pottery found
in the far corner. Since the blonde was blushing
prettily at something Monroe said, Alexis figured
they still had a little bit more time before he noticed

what they were doing.

"Charlie, help me look for a latch or pull." Alexis started gently running her hands along the doors, starting at the seam that split the two. She surmised that if part of the carving was a pull then it would most likely be near where the two doors met. Simple physics said that would be the most logical place.

After a few minutes of futile searching, Charlie sighed, "I don't think we are going to find a handle, Doc. Maybe we could pry it open."

Alexis narrowed her eyes at him, "Do you want to damage this?"

He held up his hands in defense, "Of course not...but it may be the only way to get it open. Plus, I think if we padded where we leveraged the pry bar we could minimize if not eliminate the damage."

Dr. Carmichael had to admit that Charlie's plan was a sound one. But even the slight possibility of damaging such a masterful carving had her hesitating.

"All right, Charlie. Go see if you can find something to pry this open, with and a lot of padding while you are at it. I'm going to stay here and give it another once over to see if we might have missed a hidden latch or something."

Alone with the carving, Alexis swore she saw something glint near the eyes of one of the dragon carvings. She laid her palms on either side of the carving's head and leaned in very close, but she couldn't see anything that would have shined like she saw. She had been hoping to find some sort of mechanism to spring the doors open, but that didn't look like it was going to be the case. She really didn't want to pry the doors open, but finding out if there was another chamber outweighed the damaged that might or might not occur.

Alexis leaned her forehead against the head of the dragon carving. Resigned to what they were about to do, she heaved a big sigh.

If anyone had been paying attention they would have noticed something strange when Dr. Carmichael sighed. Her exhaled breath curled like smoke and was tinged with red and orange when it touched the ancient wood. The dragon carving seemed to inhale this essence and its eyes flashed a fiery red.

Alexis felt a rumble through the great carved door. She stepped back, staring at the vibrating carvings with wide eyes. With a whoosh, the entrance to a secondary chamber opened, emitting air stale with age. The sound disturbed the rest of the dig team, and everyone, including Dr. Monroe, turned to see what the noise was.

Alexis saw Monroe heading her way out of the corner of her eye. The blonde intern was forgotten as soon as he sensed a possible new discovery. Alexis was going to be the first to enter that chamber, and any discovery therein would be listed as discovered by Dr. Carmichael—not Dr. Monroe.

His dreams began to swirl and fade. The fantastical images of his cosmic consciousness coalesced into the here and now, leaving behind the shadows of the past and the imaginings of the future.

"*Yr wyf yn?...*" He was having trouble remembering who he was, a sure sign that he had been held in stasis for too long. He forced himself to concentrate, to disentangle his sense of self from the greater universe. "*Yr wyf yn Ladon.*" His declaration ripped his consciousness from the cosmos and slammed it back into the physical realm.

Returning to consciousness was almost a painful experience. It felt as if the hand of god had physically body-slammed him into the ground. He wondered how long his mind had traveled among the neural net his nano machines had created to help keep his mind from going mad. While he knew that his body had not been disturbed since falling into his deep slumber, the world around it felt alien to him.

When his mind was fully merged with his great dragon body, he found that he still could not move. He could feel the presence of men and women outside of his chamber, but they were foreign. Their smells and minds were unknown to him. The language running around their group was not the language of his people. Had something happened to his nano machines to make them malfunction? Ladon sent his senses out trying to find someone familiar, but none of his beloved handmaidens were near. In fact, the only thing that greeted him was the smell of death and age.

For days Ladon felt the people outside in their activity. They used crude tools and did not seem to notice the microscopic machines that observed them. He took that time to slowly reintegrate into his body, moving muscles that had frozen to an almost stone-like state after who knows how many centuries. When he was not reestablishing neural pathways, he listened to the minds of those around him that his machines and attached themselves to. He learned the strange language that most of the people outside of his chamber seemed to speak. He still didn't understand many of the things their minds showed him. The people seemed much more technologically advanced then he remembered of this planet, yet they still paled in comparison to the Drako people.

Still, he wondered what had happened. Stasis was only used for emergencies, such as a fatal wound. A few chose to use stasis for long-distance travel to move live cargo. Even if he slept because of an injury, it was the duty of the handmaidens to keep the temple. They should have programmed the nano machines that controlled the stasis field to release him once his injury had healed. Ladon could find no trace of those special women who carried the DNA and nano machines of a dragoness within them, and it seemed as if many generations had passed.

Suddenly he felt her on the other side of the door—a woman who held the dragoness within. Her nanos were few, but strong. He could feel them gathering strength. Perhaps the council had sent him a new handmaiden. But sensing a single person with faint traces of shared DNA didn't explain why he was alone in this dust-filled chamber.   In the past there had been numerous handmaidens as well as other dragons. He was impatient to question the woman on the other side of the door.

The question now was if she could pass the test. The doors would open only if the nano machines within her were strong enough. She had to 'breathe fire,' releasing enough of Drako DNA combined with nanos in her breath like a key that only a handmaiden or dragon carried. If she could do that, the doors would open for her. If there wasn't enough of a nano presence, then the doors would remain firmly shut.

Ladon was almost giddy with anticipation. He felt the woman's essence through his nano machines; surprised filled him when he first connected to her. Compassion delicately balanced with a warrior's spirit...she was intoxicating and beautiful, and he hadn't even set eyes upon her yet.

The door opened and Ladon's heart roared.

Alexis shined her headlamp into the chamber beyond. On the far side was the most realistic dragon sculpture she had ever seen. It looked like a sleeping dragon curled in on itself. The body of it was red and glimmered in her lamp light. Briefly, Alexis wondered if perhaps it had been inlaid with jewels. The massive size of it would make it one of the world's wonders if it was in fact bejeweled. She swept her lamp through the chamber, noting that there didn't appear to be a sarcophagus of any sort. The lack of a king's burial disappointed her. Her eyes went back to the massive dragon sculpture. It would be a very unique find in and of itself. It was a one-of-a-kind piece. Perhaps she could still make a name for herself in the archeological world with it.

"Dr. Carmichael!" Dr. Monroe called to her as he hurried over. Alexis knew it was petty, but she wanted to be the first to enter the chamber. It was almost a compulsion. "Wait!"

Alexis ignored Monroe and stepped into the chamber, alone. She was blinded by the flames that sprang to life, illuminating the entire room. In the back of her mind she made a note to herself to figure out the parlor trick that did that. With flames flickering around her, she reached up and turned off her headlamp to conserve its battery.

Walking towards the great dragon sculpture, Alexis saw the shadows from the dancing flames play across the creation. Even though the light was fairly bright, it still made the dragon seem to be alive. If she wasn't the reasonable, educated person that she was, she would have sworn that the dragon moved. It was probably the effect that the ancients of this area wanted to project. Perhaps this was a temple complex instead of a burial site.

"Whoa…." Alexis turned at the sound of Charlie's voice. For a moment, she had forgotten that she wasn't alone here. In the doorway stood Charlie and Dr. Monroe, both of them wide eyed.

Alexis could see the wheels turning in Monroe's eyes. This was a one-of-a-kind find. Nowhere in the history of archeological sites worldwide, let alone here in Wales, had anything like this been found.

Alexis turned to stake her claim on this find when Monroe stepped into the chamber. As soon as both feet crossed the threshold, the earth began to shake and tremble. *My god!* They were in the middle of an earthquake.

Alexis had wandered deeper into the secondary chamber than she had realized. She watched in horror as stones came crashing down in the doorway. She wasn't even sure if Monroe had made it out or if he had been crushed beneath the falling stones. When the earth quit shaking, Alexis knew she wouldn't be getting out through the door she had entered because it was completely cut off by fallen debris. She hoped that no one on the dig team had been injured and that they weren't cut off from the outside like she was.

For a moment Alexis started to panic. Her breathing increased and her heart raced. Alexis squeezed her eyes shut and pinched the bridge of her nose between her fingers. Allowing herself to lose control would not help matters any. She needed to be collected and logical….

"Ni ddylech wybod dynion yn cael eu caniatáu yn y lle hwn."

Alexis whipped around trying to find the source of the deep rumbling male voice, who was apparently speaking something that sounded like Welsh. She looked over where the massive dragon statue should have been. But the jeweled creation was no longer there; in its place stood an imposing figure.

Great, now I am hallucinating, Alexis thought.

"Pam nad ydych yn ymateb, fy arglwyddes?"

Alexis just stared. At least her mind had dreamed up someone yummy. He was well over six feet tall, with flame-colored hair, just brushing his shoulders. As her eyes traveled down his body, she was greeted with wide shoulders that tapered into a narrow set of hips. His chest was bare and had the kind of muscles that made a woman's fingers itch to touch them. His long legs were clad in what appeared to be form-fitting leather braes held up by a wide tooled belt.

While his costume made him look like an extra for a Viking-age saga, the most striking thing about him was his eyes. They were an unusual gold color with flecks of red that seemed to swirl when she stared at them intently.

Alexis could see the figment of her imagination was getting frustrated at her lack of response, but somehow she felt that talking to this figment of her imagination would make her twice as crazy as just seeing him.

The man's eyes narrowed and his gaze intensified, until Alexis felt like he was trying to see into her soul.

Pain exploded behind her eyes, sending Alexis to her knees. She gripped her head and clenched her teeth to keep in the scream that wanted to escape in. If felt like clawed fingers were rifling through her brain.

After the initial shock of pain at the invasion, Alexis's logical mind kicked in. She had to get whatever this was out of her mind. The attack was mental, so she knew the defense had to be mental as well. She had to close her mind off from the thing inside of it or she was going to die. She pictured a door and physically shoved the entity in her mind out of it. Then she began building a wall, brick by brick, in front of the door.

With each brick she imagined mortaring into

her mental wall, the pressure in her head eased. But it was physically exhausting to keep the invader at bay.

She had commandeered his nano machines
with her own and shut them off. Ladon was one of
the most powerful dragon warriors the Drako had
ever known, which meant his machines fed off his
mental strength. Only one other dragon had ever
been able to mentally block him, and this little
female had successfully closed him off, even though
he felt the nano machines in her system were few
and underdeveloped. What kind of power would she
have at her full potential? Of course, despite her
surprising strength, he had the information he needed
now to communicate with her, having gleaned which
of the many languages the foreigners spoke she used

from her mind.

But still, no female had ever had the strength to oppose him before, which was one of the reasons he continued to throw himself against the barrier she erected in her mind. He was curious just how many of his machines she could shut down.

Ladon studied the woman. She was attractive, tiny in stature, but curved in all the right places. Ample breasts with generous hips, a tiny waist…all packaged in creamy white skin. Her hair was so dark that it seemed black; though he wondered why it had been shorn so short that the curls haloed around her face, barely brushing her chin. The woman he had known prized long hair as a sign of their feminity. He thought he had seen a flash of blue eyes before she shut them.

His eyes never left the woman as she collapsed, blood trickling out of her nose. He was able to reach her with inhuman speed and catch her before she hit the ground.

Ladon cursed himself. No matter her mental strength, she was still human. His test had caused her injury, something he would never forgive himself for. Women, even those that served them on this distant planet, were meant to be treasured and protected. His actions were inexcusable.

He gently wiped the blood from her face as her eyes fluttered open. They studied one another for the longest time.

"Damn, I have a really good imagination."

Ladon chuckled, a rumbling sound, like thunder, that reverberated through Alexis's body as he held her in his arms.

"I assure you, M'lady…I am not a construct of your mind." It was the same deep voice that called out to her earlier, except now he was speaking English.

Alexis gave a brief thought that she should probably panic now, but she somehow felt safe cradled in this massive man's arms.

"I apologize for the harm I have caused you."

"Hmm…what?" Alexis had been busy admiring his sculpted chest and chiseled jaw.

"I was surprised when you threw me out of your mind. Few warriors are able to withstand me, and you are but a female. I had only intended to test your strength, not cause you injury."

Just a female? Of all the arrogant, asinine things her hallucination could say to her. Alexis' eyes narrowed and she shoved him away from her. He didn't move; instead she shoved herself away from him.

"You? You were that thing in my mind?" She stood up quickly, wobbling a bit with light headedness. "How dare you invade my privacy?" She paced back and forth, ranting about privacy and arrogant men. Every once in a while she would turn to ask a question that she never stopped to listen to the answer to.

Ladon found her temper amusing. She definitely had the fire of a dragoness inside her.

"I assure that was indeed me. Though honestly I never expected you to resist the connection, none of the other handmaidens ever did. They considered accepting my nano machines as a sign of my favor." He walked over to her, reaching out to play with a curl of her hair. It was as soft as he imagined it to be.

"Handmaidens? Nano machines?" Alexis was confused, and it showed in her pursed lips that frowned slightly. Ladon had the urge to reach over and smooth the creases that appeared on her forehead as she tried to puzzle out the meaning of what he had just said.

"The Drako have always had handmaidens to see to their needs on this planet," Ladon stated matter of factly.

Alexis batted his hand away. "Drako? What is that, like some sort of warrior caste? And just what do you mean by 'this planet'?"

Ladon frowned. She had completed the ritual that opened the door to the chamber; surely she knew all of this. "Why do you tease when you have been chosen as one of the handmaidens to see to my needs?"

"Whoa bub…. Hold up." She stalked away from him and turned to face him. Her arms were crossed across her chest and her stance was rigid. "I'm nobody's handmaiden."

"You have been chosen. It is a great honor." Ladon closed the distance between the two of them. "Do not worry if you have been shamed before. As a handmaiden, you will no longer be shunned."

"Excuse me…. shamed…shunned? What the hell are you talking about?"

"Well I had assumed…why else would they chop off your hair and make you walk around dressed as a man if not to shame you."

Alexis snorted with laughter as he continued.

"Though I had wondered if perhaps you were being pursued and you were trying to disguise yourself as a boy…. Which I must tell you would be ridiculous because even dressed as a man you are obviously a beautiful woman. Of course, that would explain why a human male tried to enter this chamber knowing that anyone other than a handmaiden or a Drako would cause the nano machines to collapse the entrance to protect its secrets."

Alexis tried not to let his pronouncement of her being beautiful affect her, so she focused on his misogynist statements instead. Throwing up her hands, she declared, "Just great—not only is my hallucination insulting me, but he's a Neanderthal as well. I happen to like my short hair and I prefer pants to dresses. Just what century do you think we live in?"

"For the love of Gaia, I am not a hallucination!" Ladon bowed his head and sighed, "As far as the century…I honestly don't know at this point."

Alexis's eyes narrowed, and she studied him. Was he trying to make a fool of her? Just what game was he playing? But the longer she watched him, the more she relaxed. His shoulders were slumped like he was tired and defeated. He had felt real when he held her in his arms. What if he wasn't a figment of her imagination? Her mind swirled with the possibilities until she was dizzy.

Ladon sat down next to the wall, leaning his head back. "I don't know how long I have been here. All I know is I woke up and the world is different. So different that it seems I no longer have a place in it."

Alexis sat down next to him. "Why don't you tell me about your world and I will try to fill you in about mine."

"I have some ideas of your world from the minds of the people that have been around this chamber for the last few days, and I have several impressions from your mind as well. Though you did kick me out before I could glean too much." His head turned and he smiled at her. She noticed he had dimples when he smiled. "I'm still quite impressed by that."

"So start with the world you remember. Maybe I can understand you better then."

"I am a Drakonian...and no, it is not a warrior cast. Drako is a planet in a distant star system. Your people called us dragons." Ladon watched her. He had absorbed enough information from her mind and coupled it with her reactions during their conversation to be able to ascertain that dragons weren't a part of the everyday world any longer. Sadness clouded his eyes at the thought that perhaps he was the only dragon left. The last of his kind...at least on this planet.

"A dragon, huh? You seem kind of small to go destroying villages and eating virgins."

Ladon burst out laughing, "Just where have you gotten your information about dragons?"

"Hollywood, mostly."

He shook his head. "Well they got it all wrong."

"They usually do," Alexis smiled. She was beginning to enjoy the company of this man. "So do you have a name? I'm Alexis Carmichael."

"I am called Ladon."

"Just Ladon? No surname, like Madonna or Cher?"

"I have no idea who those people are."

"Oh yeah…you are definitely in the wrong time. So tell me the real story of dragons…at least I will get to learn something new before we die in here."

Ladon threaded his fingers through hers. He didn't know why he did it, but the feeling of needing to comfort her was just too strong. "I wouldn't let you die, Alexis."

She looked at him with a small smile that faded as soon as the lights surrounding them began to fade. "What's happening?"

"When that man stepped through the chamber door he triggered a shutdown of the nano machines sustaining this place. It is no longer sacred, and the energy is fading away. Your people aren't advanced enough to know the secrets of our technology, so the nano machines will break down into their base elements until no trace of them is found."

"You have used that term before…nano machines. Are they what it sounds like?" The flames went out entirely, leaving the pair in inky blackness. "I don't want to be in the dark." Alexis's voice rose slightly; panic was creeping in. Then she remembered her headlamp and she switched it on. The light was faint, but it was enough to see an amused smile on Ladon's face.

"Then I guess it is time to leave."

"How?"

"Through the back door." Ladon smirked at her.

Alexis punched him in the arm, "You jerk….

You mean we could have left at any time?"

"Pretty much."

Ladon stood and pulled Alexis to her feet. "Lead on good sir."

*****

At the back of the chamber Ladon showed Alexis a large carved stone. It depicted four dragons circling each other around what appeared to be a representation of the tree of life.

"This covers the way out."

Alexis walked over to the carving and leaned her back against it. Bracing her feet on the floor for traction, she shoved the stone with everything she had. She attempted to push the stone out of the way and it wouldn't budge even an inch. Ladon looked to be a very powerful man, but even so Alexis didn't see how they were going to move the stone.

"I think we are still stuck here." Alexis looked over to Ladon to see him chuckling at her attempt to move the stone. His laughter just pissed her off. Alexis crossed her arms and scowled at him. "You think you can do any better?"

"As a matter of fact…" Ladon grabbed

Alexis by the shoulders and directed her to stand some distance away from the stone. Alexis waited, thinking up numerous amusing quips she could fire off at him once he failed to move the stone. Because no matter how powerful a man he was, they needed a forklift to get that stone out of the way.

Ladon inhaled, then exhaled and just stood there in front of the stone. He appeared to be doing some sort of meditative breathing. His backside was a nice sight. Alexis snorted. Meditation wasn't going to move the stone, and she was just about to speak up to tell him so when the air around Ladon seemed to shimmer.

Ladon's body began to contort, muscles bulging, bones popping, his entire being growing exponentially in size, until he seemed to fill that end of the chamber. As he grew, his clothing seemed to melt away, leaving Alexis with an impressive view for a short time until his body began to change. His hands sharpened into taloned claws. His face elongated as huge teeth burst forth. Then suddenly the growth stopped and for just a moment it seemed like time had stopped and Ladon would forever be confined to the frightening deformed giant before her. Starting at his snout, the pale, stretched skin of humanity changed like a cascading wave of color. Scales in various shades of deep, rich red emerged, rippling down his skin, until not a trace of his humanity remained; before her stood a powerful, bejeweled red dragon.

Alexis's hands flew to her mouth to contain the scream that was threatening to burst forth from her body. Her eyes were wide with terror. She had truly lost it. She had to be stuck in some nightmare. That was the only explanation. Dragons from other planets just didn't exist. Maybe a stone fell on her when the earthquake hit and she was at some hospital in a coma.

This is reality whether you choose to accept it or not. A deep rumbling voice filled her mind. She would recognize that voice anywhere.

"Shit…you really are a dragon!" She could feel him chuckling in her psyche. Alexis looked Ladon over from nose to tail; there was something familiar about him. "Oh my god! You were the jewel encrusted dragon statue I saw from the doorway."

It was all too much to take in, and Alexis ended up doing something she had never done in her entire life. She fainted.

*****

Ladon looked at where Alexis crumpled to

the ground. He noticed the gentle rise and fall of her chest and, reassured that she had only fainted, turned back to the problem at hand. He might have been able to move the stone in his human form, because even in that form he was much more powerful than any human being. But he had decided to transform.

If he was honest with himself, he transformed not because it would make escape easier, though it did do that. No, he transformed because for some reason he wanted Alexis to know all of him and accept him as he was, no pretense. His heart constricted a bit that she had fainted. To him that told him that she couldn't handle him as he was. So now he had to make a painful decision.

In all his life he had never been drawn to a single female. Oh, he had tumbled a few and had his carnal needs met. That was, after all, one of the roles of the handmaidens who had once served his kind. But in all his numerous years he never wanted to claim just one. It had shocked him that, in a single day, that was exactly what he wanted to do to Alexis. He tried to rationalize his feelings as a side effect of invading her mind. True, he hadn't seen everything about her, but he saw enough to be awed at the kind of person she was. She had earned even more of his respect when she had forced him from her mind.

Alexis was most assuredly unique. But no matter how much he wanted to, Ladon would not claim a woman who could not accept the dragon part of himself. No Drako warrior would live a half-life without his dragon. So it was with a heavy heart that he rolled the stone away, revealing the hidden tunnel that would lead them to the world outside. Their little interlude had come to an end.

He took his time transforming himself back into his human appearance. Even with his decision made, he was reluctant to leave because leaving meant not seeing the spunky little Alexis again and that saddened him. He tried to rationalize that it was just because he felt a connection to her in this foreign world. Shaking his head to banish his musings, he moved towards her. Ladon picked Alexis up and gently cradled her to his chest. Even in her unconscious state she snuggled closer to his protective warmth.

With every step, Ladon left his old life behind. The dragons didn't seem to be a part of this new Earth. Ladon had to discover if he could find a way to call his home world. He also wondered if his own planet had changed as much as this one. If he could not contact his home, could he forge a place for himself in this new reality? He had much to learn; many things had changed in the centuries he had slumbered in this chamber. But more than anything, he had to find out if any others of his kind had survived on this planet.

Ladon blinked at the brightness of the sun as he stepped out of the tunnel. He could hear frantic voices on the far side of the cairn. Knowing that Alexis would soon be discovered, he laid her gently on the ground just outside of the tunnel. He leaned towards her and kissed her forehead. Then Ladon turned and walked away, disappearing from her life.

A knock sounded on Dr. Carmichael's office door.

"Hey, that golden Welsh horde is being displayed at the Kimbell Museum of Art. Want to go with me?" Marcy, Alexis's teaching assistant, popped her head in the door.

"No, thank you. I have too much work to get caught up on. I have to finish writing up the final exams." Marcy waved goodbye and left.

Alexis wasn't about to tell Marcy that she had been there when the horde was discovered. Once again Dr. Monroe had swooped in and taken credit for her hard work. Of course, it hadn't helped that when they found her she was babbling about dragons and aliens. The university, worried about traumatic brain injury from the cave in, had felt that it would be best to list Monroe as the primary university representative on the dig. Of course, since Alexis refused to sleep with him again, he had made sure that her name was left out of all the major papers.

Between Monroe cutting her out of any recognition on the find and reporting back to the university about her dragon 'hallucination,' Alexis's professional reputation had been in ruins. This was how she found herself teaching history at a little college in Ft. Worth, Texas. She didn't mind the work, but she despaired of ever getting a place on another respectable dig. Field work had been where Alexis Carmichael's heart really was. But recently, she had resigned herself to being only a simple history professor.

It did irk her that Dr. Monroe had somehow figured out a way to stretch his fifteen minutes of fame into five years of glory. The Welsh horde was giving King Tut a run for its money as far as drawing crowds to museums, which is why it had been on tour pretty much nonstop the last few years.

Alexis often wondered if she actually did have some sort of traumatic experience, since she woke outside the chamber and Ladon had disappeared. She made a mistake when she had tried to explain to Charlie what had happened to her; she had been honest. That honesty had cost her everything.

Sighing, Alexis switched off her laptop and shoved it into her bag. She was too keyed up to concentrate on her work, so she would have to take it home with her and hopefully get it done there.

She was walking out the door when her office phone rang. She debated letting it just go to voicemail, but the only people who called her on that line were her department heads and students needing to make an appointment to see her. She set her bag on the chair and picked up the phone.

"Hello, Dr. Carmichael speaking."

"Hello, Alexis."

Alexis Carmichael sank to the floor. She would know that deep rumbling voice anywhere. She had almost convinced herself that he didn't actually exist. But here he was, reappearing in her life five years later.

"Ladon." She breathed his name in a whisper. This man who had haunted her dreams even after ruining her life—she had never been able to forget him.

*****

Ladon had spent the last five years making a place for himself in this new era. He quickly rose in station as he increased his wealth. It wasn't difficult. As a dragon, he had the ability to use his nano machines to harmonize with the world around him. He was especially tuned to the earth and fire. This allowed him to find resources that many others wouldn't be able to find. Using his vast stores of strength, he had been able self-replicate numerous machines in his body even without having access to a Drako ship. He used these machines to pull precious metals and gems to the surface, giving him the stake he needed to create his identity.

His first order of business had been to find someone with the ability to forge a new identity for him, because he had quickly discovered that in this day and age a person was not identified by the stories of their glory sung around the bonfire, but by massive amounts of bureaucratic paperwork. Some things didn't change as civilizations advanced; bureaucracy was one of them. He also found that little had changed about humanity. Everyone seemed to have a price.

He became Ladon Drake, heir to a mining fortune, businessman, playboy. It was a good image. It allowed him into the highest circles of society and gave him the backing to have most anyone jumping at his beck and call.

Once his companies had grown from small mining operations to boardroom meetings and multiple companies, Ladon had been able to use his mental abilities to stay one step ahead of his competition. The battle arena may have changed throughout the centuries, but there were always enemies that needed to be outmaneuvered, and he was still the best when it came to winning.

He used his new-found wealth and status in society to search for any other remaining dragons. So far he had only awakened one other dragon that had guarded a vast library of information in the East. It was this library that he hoped might lead them to more of their brethren.

Unfortunately, research and sifting through historical clues was not his forte; which is why he was on the phone with Alexis Carmichael. She had the knowledge he needed and already knew about the Drako. She was the logical choice for this job. At least that is what he kept telling himself.

Truth is, he had never been able to banish her from his thoughts. He followed her life from afar. He knew about her troubles and many times wanted to swoop in and save her. But he never did.

"I need your help, Alexis."

"Five years, Ladon.... You disappear the day I met you and decide to call me up out of the blue to ask for help?" Alexis's voice was almost a growl at this point. "Give me one good reason why I should help you?"

"Because you are the only one who can...."

"Damn it, Ladon. My life fell apart after meeting you. I have a feeling it would be even worse this time."

"I need an archeologist, Alexis.... I need you."

"There are hundreds of archeologists you could employ. Why me?"

"You know why."

Alexis sighed and pinched the bridge of her nose with her fingers. "I don't want to get involved with that again."

"Alexis…have lunch with me. Hear me out. If you decide to walk away after that I will let you go and you will never see me again."

Alexis knew that she would live to regret this, but ever since meeting Ladon she had felt like she was missing something vital. Perhaps if she confronted him she would find that missing piece again.

"Fine…when?"

Ladon let out a relieved breath, "I'll be in Ft. Worth in two days. I'll pick you up at the college around noon."

"You had better make it one. I have a class that isn't finished until 12:30."

"Deal…. I'll see you soon."

Ladon hung up the phone feeling both relieved and nervous.

"You've got that look on your face again."
Ladon looked over to Ryuu. He was the dragon that
Ladon had discovered in the ancient library.
Compared to Ladon, he was the scholarly sort and
rarely spoke unless he had something to say, though
he didn't look like a scholar. Like most dragons, he
looked like an ancient warrior. Ryuu was at least six
and a half feet tall. Where Ladon's coloring was in
shades of red, Ryuu was all black: black hair with
eyes so dark they appeared black. His dragon state
was a great obsidian beast.

"I told you I can do the research myself."
Ryuu crossed his arms over his chest and glared at
Ladon. "It is my library after all."

"I know you are more than capable of finding
the information. But I have a feeling our time is
short and an extra set of eyes would make the work
go by that much faster. We need to discover why we
slept, if there are any others of our kind left, and,
most importantly, why we can't communicate with
our home world." Ladon turned his desk chair to
face Ryuu. They were in the offices of Draco
International, the company Ladon had formed. He
had started out as a small mining operation, but in
short order had diversified the company to be a
power player in many international markets. The
office had been decorated in a Zen-like design.
Ladon still preferred natural materials to the
synthetic ones popular in today's society, so natural
wood and stone were everywhere.

"Why this woman?" Ryuu was like a dog
with a bone. Since Ladon had suggested contacting
Alexis for help Ryuu had been asking the same
questions.

"We've been over this…she knows about us.
So she is the logical choice." Ladon stood up from
his chair and paced in front of the floor-to-ceiling

windows that made up one wall of his office. He didn't even notice the view of the Rocky Mountains. When Ladon had left Wales, he traveled to what is now known as the United States. In earlier times, this land had been the refuge of many dragons. The native populations were sparse, with vast tracks of land that no man traversed. It was a place of solitude and meditation. Ladon watched the people scurry between the numerous buildings that had taken over the peaceful landscape. He couldn't help but muse how things had changed.

Ryuu laid a hand on Ladon's shoulder, "It isn't just her qualifications…your voice changes when you speak about her and you get a look in your eyes like you are no longer really here. You can lie to me if you want about this woman, but do not lie to yourself."

Ladon laid his head against the cool glass; snow would be falling soon in the Rockies. "If I knew what she was to me I would tell you. I knew her for one day, but somehow she is never far from my thoughts."

"Could she be your true mate?"

Ladon snorted. "Do you still believe in that fairy tale? Never once have I encountered a true mate pair. Females were so rare on our home world that many Drako males attached themselves to anyone that would have them. Every dragon warrior stationed here had numerous handmaidens to see to their needs, and never did they feel the need to cleave themselves to just one of them, even when such couplings produced offspring."

"That is not entirely true. What about Hathor?"

"That was obsession."

"Zoya? She was human and she was a true mate."

Ladon shook his head. "Her mate loved her, this is true, but I doubt they were really true mates. Tugarin never displayed any mystical powers."

Ryuu went over to the wet bar on the other side of the office. He pulled out a tumbler and poured himself some bourbon. "The sagas are filled with stories of bonded pairs and the power that comes with such a connection."

"And modern Hollywood is filled with Cinderella stories, but how often does the poor girl snag the rich man and live happily ever after?"

"Point taken…but you still have some sort of connection; otherwise you wouldn't be mooning over her five years after a single meeting. Maybe you just need sex." Ryuu threw back the bourbon and downed it in one gulp.

"I haven't exactly been a saint these last five years you know." Ladon turned to face Ryuu, leaning his back against the chilled planes of glass. "It just feels empty. There is no joy in it."

Ryuu whistled low. "No joy in sex…are you sure you are feeling okay, man?"

Ladon shrugged. "To be honest, I don't know. Everything has changed since I woke up. I don't like not knowing my place in the world."

"We will create a new place for ourselves if that is necessary." Ryuu placed the empty glass in the small sink of the wet bar. The cleaning service would get it later. "You are understandably restless after hibernating for centuries. You spent more time amongst the nano machines as pure thought than you did in this mortal realm. That experience changed us. But I think you need to figure out what it is about this woman that has you obsessing."

"It may not matter if I can't convince her to help us." Ladon sighed as he walked over to his desk chair and slumped into it.

Ryuu shrugged, slipping into one of the chairs across from Ladon's desk. "I think that is going to be the easy part. I've read the reports on her. She was a driven researcher until she discovered you. With the digging I have done, her being pushed out of field work wasn't her choice. A passion like that doesn't die. You know our library is a unique find. Even if she isn't allowed to publish any of its history, the scholar in her would want to see it.

The question is, what will you do once you have her here?"

"Seduce her with knowledge." Ladon quirked a brow up and gave Ryuu a mischievous grin. He already had a plan forming. Perhaps the reason he couldn't get her out of his mind was because there was a sexual attraction between them. Ladon figured once the mystery of how well they went together in the bedroom was solved that Alexis would lose some of her allure. After all, men always want what they can't have. Dragons aren't much different.

It was now half past one o'clock. Alexis didn't understand why she was so nervous to see Ladon again. After all, his stupid ass was the reason she lost her creditability in her field. She should be out working on some major dig, not grading papers at some dinky little college. Of course, it was the papers she was blaming for her tardiness, but the truth was she wasn't sure she could face the man…dragon…whatever…that ruined her life.

Alexis couldn't deny the shiver of awareness that went through her body. Without even looking up, she knew he was standing in the doorway of her office.

"You're late."

"I'm working. Perhaps it would be better if we rescheduled." Alexis gestured to the piles of papers on her desk. "As you can see I am kind of swamped."

Ladon leaned over, placing both hands on her desk. He was so close she could feel his heat. He smelled of cinnamon and man. He had cut his hair. She liked it shorter; there was this curl that draped over his forehead that her hands were just itching to touch. Damn! She didn't want to be attracted to him. She had hoped that the dreams and fantasies that had plagued her these last few years were fabrications of her mind blown out of proportion. But now she was faced with the hard reality that, if anything, her dreams fell far short of the actual man standing in front of her.

"One hour, Alexis. That's all I'm asking. Give me one hour to explain why I am here. If at the end of that hour you want me out of your life, I will go. No questions asked. Can you do that for me?"

"One hour and you will leave me alone?" Alexis chewed on her lip as she thought. She could make it through one hour, right? "Fine. Start talking, bub. The clock is ticking down."

Ladon was about to launch into his rehearsed pitch about the dragon library when a student burst into the office.

"Oh, sorry Dr. Carmichael. I didn't know you were in a meeting." The young man plopped a paper on Alexis's desk. "Here's my thesis." He turned and scurried out the door.

No sooner had the door closed, and Ladon was about to commence, then it opened yet again; this time a young woman was asking for help locating sources about a particular archeological study. After a third and fourth student interrupted them, Ladon realized that there was no way he would be able to talk to Alexis if they remained here.

"Have you had lunch?"

"What?"

"Lunch...you know food, midday meal."

"I know what lunch is. Why do you ask?"

"Because I can't bloody talk to you here with all of these interruptions." Ladon scowled at the door, and Alexis had to suppress a giggle at his disgruntled face.

"Well some of us have to work for a living, Mr. Moneybags"

Ladon's eyes snapped to Alexis's face.

"No, I haven't been stalking you. But I have had to schmooze enough with big money at university functions to know that your shoes alone probably cost more than I make in a month. So I would say you have done well for yourself."

Ladon coughed. "I had a few tricks I could pull to get me started."

"I have no doubt." Alexis turned off her computer and stood up, throwing her purse over one shoulder. "I believe you said something about food. Just so you know, you are buying." She skirted her desk and practically gave Ladon a heart attack when he saw that she wore a form-fitting grey wool pencil skirt.

"Yes, ma'am." Ladon followed Alexis out the door, keeping his eyes on the delicious view of her swaying backside. He began humming the eighties tune 'Hot for Teacher' as they exited the building.

*****

Alexis had directed Ladon to a little hole-in-the-wall Mexican restaurant in one of the more rundown neighborhoods in Ft. Worth. As Ladon stepped out of the little Audi he had rented for this trip, he wondered if it would still have tires and a stereo by the time their lunch was over. Ladon had spent as little time as possible in the poor and working-class levels as he could. He demanded certain luxuries in life. Alexis, however, seemed quite comfortable here, calling out greetings in Spanish to the old man sitting on the stoop of a house across the street from the restaurant.

"Are you sure it is safe to eat here?" Ladon eyed the peeling paint and cracked stucco of the building in front of them. Stray cats scurried around the dumpster at the back of the parking lot. Hopefully they didn't end up on the menu as well.

"This place has the best chile rellenos this side of the Rio Grande." Alexis looked over the building, seeing it through a stranger's eyes. "Manuel's parents run this place. It may not look like much, but his mother is one of the best cooks you will ever meet."

Ladon's heart stopped when Alexis mentioned another male's name. She was a beautiful woman; he shouldn't be surprised that she had other men in her life. But it still felt like someone stabbed him in the gut.

Alexis led Ladon through the door into the dim interior where, mariachi music played over the speakers placed around the restaurant. The tables and chairs were all mismatched, but the place was spotless and the aromas drifting from the kitchen made his mouth water. The patrons lifted their heads and Ladon realized that he and Alexis were perhaps the only Caucasians in the entire place. It made Ladon feel like he was an intruder in this place.

As the door closed with a tingle of the bell suspended above it, a plump little Mexican woman popped her head out of the door he assumed went to the kitchen. When she spotted Alexis, her face lit up and the mamacita with streaks of grey in her hair squealed before running over to embrace Alexis in a flurry of Spanish. That reaction seemed to be good enough for the rest of the crowd, since they all turned back to their meals without a word.

She led them over to a table near the kitchens and disappeared again. Ladon picked up a menu to look over the selections when he felt Alexis' small hand on his arm. He looked up and saw her shake her head and gesture at the menu. He gave her a dubious look and she mouthed, "trust me."

Shrugging, he laid the menu aside when a boy of maybe ten delivered fresh tortilla chips with queso and guacamole.

"Gracias, Manuel." The little boy smiled and scurried away without a word.

"So that was Manuel? Somehow I thought he might have been older?"

"So what if he had been? You have no claim on me, Ladon." Alexis snatched a chip and scooped a heaping portion of guacamole onto it before popping it in her mouth.

"So how did you find this place?" Ladon dipped a chip in the queso and took a bite, almost moaning in pleasure. *Oh god, that is some good food.* He had never tasted anything like it, and this was just the appetizer.

Alexis shrugged, "I make extra money tutoring ESL students for the public-school systems."

"ESL?"

"English as a second language." Ladon nodded and motioned for her to continue. "Since I am familiar with a fair range of different languages, it seemed like an easy way to supplement the meager salary I make teaching." Ladon felt a bit guilty and wondered if her financial hardship was because of what happened after meeting him. "Manuel was one of my students. The first time he ever made the honor roll at school, Mrs. Rodriguez, his mom, made me a batch of tamales as a thank you. They were so wonderful I asked if I could purchase more of them and we struck up a friendship, which led me here."

Ladon was about to say something when Mrs. Rodriguez appeared carrying numerous plates of food. It surprised Ladon that even though he hadn't ordered anything specific that the woman seemed to know exactly what he had wanted. He looked up at Alexis with wide eyes before digging into the scrumptious food.

"I told you so," was all Alexis said before she dug into her own plate of food.

Half an hour later Ladon leaned back into his chair and rubbed his full stomach, "How did she do that?"

Alexis chuckled, "Rumor has it that Mrs. Rodriguez is a bruja, a witch. She always knows just what a person wants to eat. Personally, I think she is just a really good cook and whatever she serves you you're going to want." She pushed the plate of sopapillas to the center of the table. "You have about half an hour left to explain to me why you are here, Ladon."

"I told you that I needed your help. I have been trying to find out if any other dragons survived the way I did. Overall, I didn't have much luck, until about a year ago. I discovered and bought a tiny uninhabited island off the coast of Japan."

"Whoa, wait a minute…you bought an entire island? Just how much money do you have?"

Ladon gave her a boyish grin, "Well it was only a small island." Alexis rolled her eyes at him. "Anyway…the mountain on this island actually had a dragon temple complex carved into it. At the heart of that I found Ryuu."

"What is Ryuu?"

"Not what…who. Ryuu is another dragon. In fact, he is the only other dragon I have found so far. He had mysteriously fallen into a deep sleep just as I had, and when I woke him he was all alone. All of the scholars and handmaidens that should have been there were gone, just like with me."

"Scholars?" Alexis picked up on that word quickly. Her time with Ladon might not have been long, but when they had met he had never asked about scholars, only his handmaidens. "Why would he expect scholars to be there?"

Ladon took a deep breath; this was the part that would either hook Alexis' interest or not. If it didn't, he would be walking out of her life permanently this afternoon. He really didn't want to do that. He might not understand why, but he knew he didn't want his time to end so suddenly with Alexis.

"He expected it because he was the keeper of the Drakonian library; its stores of knowledge surpassed even the library at Alexandria."

Alexis tapped her chin, eyes downcast, mentally calculating something. When she looked up at Ladon, he could see her eyes sparkling with curiosity and perhaps avarice.

"Does the library still exist?"

"Alexis," there was a warning in Ladon's voice, "This isn't something you can write about. This modern world thinks dragons are a myth, and until we figure out why that is, it needs to stay that way."

"Then why are you telling me about it?"

"Because we are hoping that there are clues in the library that can help us locate others and maybe even figure out what happened to us. Ryuu is a great scholar, but it will take him years to get through this alone. You already know about us and have the credentials to help."

Alexis frown at him, "You are asking me to give up my entire life to help you in one of the greatest archeological research projects, but I can't publish anything I find. Are you insane?"

"I know it doesn't seem like a fair trade."

"It's not…. I may not have the career I want, but if I take a break from what I do have without anything to show for it, then my career is as good as dead, Ladon. I've worked too hard to rebuild what I have."

"What if Draco International hired you as a consultant? We have a lot of different properties, some of which may have archeological significance. You would be paid a salary, which is more generous than what you are making now teaching. You would have to sign off on a few papers while others did the leg work on those projects, leaving you free to work with us on the library."

Alexis ripped off the corner of one the sopapillas she had abandoned earlier and dipped it into honey. She was thoughtful as she popped the morsel in her mouth and chewed. What he was offering her sounded fair. She wouldn't have any unexplained gaps in employment and technically she would be involved in some digs and research, even if it was only on paper, which was more than she had now. The increase in pay would be nice, and it wasn't like she was leaving behind family here in Ft. Worth.

So why was she stalling? This might be the thing that gets her back in the field. Alexis knew that her hesitancy had more to do with the man sitting across from her than the job offer itself. Any way she looked at it; Ladon still had the power to get under her skin. If she was hung up on him this much five years later after a single day, what was she going to feel after working with him day after day?

"Please say yes, Alexis…. I need you."

She knew that it was probably her own deluded heart, but Alexis thought she heard more in that simple statement. Maybe Ladon had been affected as much as she had by their meeting years ago. She would never know for certain if she didn't take a chance now.

"All right, Ladon. I'll help." Alexis hoped she wasn't dooming her heart in the process.

"Great, I can have your things stored and we

can make arrangements for travel by the end of next week…"

"Whoa, not so fast there, Speedy. I do have a life here, and considering how long it took me to get the job here; I'd rather not burn any bridges along the way. The semester ends in a couple of weeks, but I still need to see if I can get a leave of absence approved."

"Oh it will be approved." Ladon smiled a predatory smile.

Damn the man! He wiggles his little fingers, throws a bit of money and everything falls into place for him. The chancellor not only approved her leave of absence, but pushed her to take time off before the end of the semester, assuring her that the department would cover her finals and the teaching assistants were capable of getting her grades in.

Alexis was seriously worried she wouldn't have a job to come back to with her boss's enthusiastic removal of her from her classroom. She found out later from the department secretary that Mr. Drake not only agreed to fund two research grants if he could borrow her for a while, but had sweetened the pot with a new science lab if he could have her within the next few days.

So now Alexis was standing on the tarmac of the private section of Love field waiting to board Ladon's private jet. They would layover in Colorado to pick up his partner, who evidently was another dragon. After that they would be heading straight to the island off Japan's coast where the dragon library lay buried.

Despite his underhanded methods, Alexis was excited about getting back into the field. She may not be able to publish her findings with the library, but having her name on active digs was still a good thing. She made a mental note to get information on the digs she was supposed to be signing off on before they went to what she assumed would be a primitive sight in Asia.

"Dr. Carmichael?"

An attractive blonde in a sharp-looking stewardess uniform walked over to Alexis.

"Yes?"

"Mr. Drake is expecting you. If you would follow me." The woman walked ahead of Alexis with what she assumed men would consider a seductive sway of the hips. Alexis couldn't help the little green-eyed monster that popped up as she thought about her own disheveled appearance compared to the polished blonde.

What did she care if Ladon surrounded himself with a veritable harem of attractive women? She was here to work nothing else. At least that was what she was telling herself.

*****

The flight from Dallas/Ft. Worth to Denver only took about an hour. When they touched down Ladon had told Alexis to not worry about their bags as they would be boarding the overseas flight that night and his staff would see to it that their baggage would be taken care of. He then rushed her off to the downtown office where his company was headquartered.

After a dizzying round of introductions and piles of contact information for the archeological teams she would be overwriting, Alexis found herself in a conference room across the table from a dour-faced man Ladon had introduced as Ryuu Mizushima.

The man had his arms crossed and was just staring silently at Alexis. Alexis took the opportunity to observe him right back. He was a large, muscular man, just like Ladon was, but that was where any similarities ended. Ryuu was dark. His hair was so black that it shined with blue highlights in the light. His skin was olive in complexion. It was difficult to determine race. His features had a somewhat Asian appearance to them, but none of the definitive features like almond shaped eyes. His eyes were just as unusual as Ladon's were, but in a different way. Where Ladon's eyes were golden with a hint of red within them, Ryuu's eyes appeared black. The irises were so dark it was difficult to tell where the pupil ended and the iris began. It gave him a disconcerting stare.

Finally, Alexis had had enough.

"What seems to be your problem with me? You obviously don't like me, and since I have been here less than a day, I can't think it is because I have done something to insult you. So, what is it?"

The corner of Ryuu's mouth quirked up just a bit; Alexis might have missed it if she hadn't been watching him so intently. At least the hulking man wasn't completely unfeeling.

"I'm trying to figure out why Ladon thinks I need you in *my* library."

The emphasis on "my"—his huge stature and slightly alien looks—the pieces of the puzzle started falling into place for Alexis. Finally, it clicked, this was the Ryuu that Ladon had talked about earlier.

"You're a dragon as well, aren't you?" Ryuu simply nodded.

"I suppose you aren't too happy having a human scholar rummaging through your library."

"I have nothing against human scholars. I was friends with many in my time."

Alexis smirked, "So it is just this human scholar you have an issue with then?"

Ryuu finally relaxed his arms somewhat, and a ghost of a smile crossed his features. "Ladon said you were a bit of a spitfire."

"It would probably be best if we steered clear of what Ladon and I would say about each other."

Ryuu let out a loud guffaw, "M'lady, I think it is going to be very entertaining having you around."

After breaking the ice, Ryuu and Alexis fell
into easy conversation. Ladon entered the
conference room to hear Alexis laugh at something
Ryuu had said. When she noticed Ladon, the smile
that had been on her lips fell into a frown. The loss
of her warm smile hit Ladon like a physical blow. It
was obvious she did not think well of him, and for
some reason that fact mattered to him.

Ladon could see Ryuu smirking over
Alexis's head. Ladon's temper flared red hot and he
really wished he could smash that smug look off of
Ryuu's face.

It wasn't until that moment that Ladon

realized that Ryuu and Alexis might have much more in common than him and Alexis. What would he do if she fell for the other dragon? Ladon mentally punched himself. What did it matter if she fell for Ryuu? Ladon wanted her here just to get her out of his system anyway. If she and Ryuu got together after he had bedded her then so be it.

"Are we ready to go? The pilot is on standby waiting for us." Ladon forced himself to smile politely.

"Give me a minute to refresh myself and I will meet you at the car." Alexis brushed by Ladon on her way to the restroom. He closed his eyes and inhaled her scent; a sweet mix of vanilla and something that was uniquely Alexis.

When the door to the conference room clicked shut, Ladon squared off with Ryuu.

"What the hell was that about?" Ladon demanded. "She's mine."

Ryuu held his hands up in mock surrender, "Alexis is a charming woman and we were having a nice conversation. Nothing more."

Ladon's brow furrowed as he took a step back from his friend. "Fine."

Ryuu watched as Ladon got himself back under control. The man was an idiot if he thought sex was the cure to what ailed him. The tension between Ladon and Alexis had been palatable. Their feelings ran a lot deeper than either one of them cared to admit.

Ryuu mentally rubbed his hands together in glee. He might come off as a stogy old scholar, but he still had a strong sense of mischief, and this thing between Ladon and Alexis was going to be full of entertaining possibilities.

The men gathered up their bags and headed for the door. Ryuu was the first to reach to it.

"You know I think I am going to like working with Dr. Carmichael. Alexis is quite charming and beautiful. Any man would be lucky to be spending time with her." The comment was tossed casually over his shoulder, but Ryuu knew that it had hit its mark when he heard Ladon growl behind him. With a chuckle, the black dragon quickly slipped out the door and headed to the elevator, where Alexis was already standing. He had to suppress a laugh when Alexis pushed the button to close the doors before Ladon could join them in the ride to the parking garage. Yup, this trip was definitely going to be entertaining.

*****

Ladon's mood only got worse during the flight to Asia. If it wasn't for the fact that he actually liked Ryuu and he was the only other living dragon as far as they knew; Ladon would have barbequed him mid-flight.

Alexis was leaning forward to hear what Ryuu was saying about the archeological digs that, up until they had hired Alexis, he had been overseeing. Their heads were together, so close that if she turned her face up just a little Ryuu could kiss her.

Ladon snorted at that thought and shifted in his seat yet again. He tried looking out the window, but there was nothing to look at but clouds. He tried to sleep, but the pair sharing the cabin of the company jet with him just made too much noise for him to get any sleep.

Okay, maybe that was an exaggeration, but damn it, he was hyper tuned to the woman. Why couldn't she smile at him like she was smiling at that stupid black dragon?

Almost as if his thoughts conjured her response, Alexis looked up at him, smiling. Her grin disintegrated in the face of his scowling. For a moment, confusion flashed across her face, quickly followed by hurt and then anger.

Fuck! (Such a good modern word for so many situations.) If he didn't get his emotions under control he was going to push her away. That would make this entire enterprise pointless. Yeah, he had told Ryuu that she would help researching the library, which is true. But now that she was on the plane crossing oceans to spend time with him, Ladon could admit that the main reason he suggested this course was he wanted her with him. She got under his skin somehow. He didn't know why, but he couldn't let her go until he investigated this attraction fully.

Ladon wiped a hand across his face and ran fingers through his hair. He closed his eyes and took a deep breath. Maybe he spent too much time out of body, because he didn't feel like himself since waking up. Of course, waking and meeting Alexis occurred almost at the same time so he couldn't pinpoint the catalyst for his present state.

His sour mood was contagious, evidently, because the only sound in the plane's cabin was the hum of the jet engine. Alexis had curled up in her chair and seemed to be trying to sleep. Ryuu was glaring at him, and when Ladon made eye contact, the black dragon mouthed, "What the hell?"

Ladon just shook his head and shrugged. Leaning back in his seat, he closed his eyes to try and catch an hour or two of sleep before they landed. Maybe he would be in a better mood after a nap.

The air was balmy when the trio stepped off the plane. They had landed on the small private airstrip that Ladon had built when he bought Wakahisa Island. The island itself was quite small, barely three miles long by two miles wide. On the east end, a single mountain rose to the sky. The side facing the rest of the island slopped gently down into a lush forest. The side of the mountain facing the sea was a sheer cliff that looked as if god had cut the island from another piece of land. No person had lived on the island for generations, which was why people questioned what a wealthy man would want with such a primitive place. Ladon had convinced them that he was wanting to build a secluded vacation home on the island, which seemed to satisfy them enough to complete the transaction.

If it had just been Ladon and Ryuu, they would have simply transformed once their plane had left for the mainland and flown up to the entrance of the library that was hidden on the cliff side of Wakahisa Mountain. But with Alexis in tow they were going to have to hike and climb to get to the dragon library.

Ladon wondered if the trek would be too physically demanding for Alexis, since many parts required someone who was an experienced rock climber to scale. He needn't have worried. Alexis seemed to blossom under the adverse conditions. Her cheeks glowed from the physical activity, making her even more beautiful. She did this little jig every time she made it through a particularly difficult area. Her smile rivaled the sun.

It was during one of those moments when Ladon watched her joy at completing a task that he had the sudden revelation of just how much she had lost in the last few years. She was meant to be exploring the wilds, not locked up in some office.

He knew that the blame for her downfall could be laid at his feet. He may not have the specifics of what happened, but he did enough digging to hear the rumors about her "mental breakdown" where she hallucinated about dragons, aliens and statues that weren't there. She actually saw a dragon…him, and he was an alien. She wasn't hallucinating. Of course, relating her experience to others who weren't there sounded like fantasy.

If nothing else, Ladon wanted to make right the things that had gone wrong in Alexis Carmichael's life because of him. That thought startled him. He wasn't known for being too concerned with others. Ryuu was the closest thing he had to a friend, and that relationship worked only because the other dragon was as solitary and self-sufficient as Ladon. But even with the thought being out of character for Ladon, he was strangely comfortable with it. He wanted to make Alexis's life better, even if it meant sacrifices in his own.

Ladon continued staring up at Alexis during this earth-shattering revelation until Ryuu elbowed him with a pointed look. The black dragon passed the red one to stand beside Alexis at the summit. Ladon seriously considered pushing his friend off the cliff. After all, it wouldn't kill him, the bastard could fly.

13

The sun was setting when the trio finally could rappel down the cliff to the hidden opening of the library. Ladon drew Alexis off to one side, away from Ryuu. This may be Ryuu's library, but Ladon found he wanted to show Alexis its wonders himself.

As the evening sun reached the horizon, it was at the perfect level to reach the first in a series of mirrors strategically placed around the interior. For a few minutes, the entire library was revealed in a blaze of golden light.

Alexis gasped at the sheer enormity of the structure within. It seemed to take up the entire mountain.

Ladon laid his hands on Alexis's shoulders and leaned in to whisper in her ear. "In ancient times that flash of light was the indication to the handmaidens within to activate the nano machines to illuminate the various crystals that provided evening light." Ladon pointed at a carved crystal near the entrance. "These are sun stones that would glow to light the interior. A similar idea to your light bulb, I believe. They didn't want to use torches or oil lamps here. Too many of the manuscripts were made of fragile paper and vellum; many were one-of-a-kind works of art. The dragons had enough worries that the young dragons would lose control of their element and do damage. They certainly wanted to keep the number of flames to a minimum. So the library is filled with crystals infused with bioluminescent nano machines." He chuckled.

Alexis couldn't help it; she smiled. In her mind's eye, she could see rambunctious young men with what seemed like magical powers running amok.

"Needless to say, the handmaidens had their hands full," Ryuu joined the pair. "Unfortunately without the handmaidens, the energy in these crystals has long since faded." The black dragon went to an alcove where he and Ladon had stashed electric lanterns and some flashlights. "Ladon says that a small crew will be here to wire some lights through the complex. Until then, we will use these. We did put lights and a generator in a couple of the sleeping quarters on the level above this one. Let's go get settled in and get some sleep so we can start in the morning."

Alexis was about to protest that she wanted to get started right away and that sleep could wait. But when she opened her mouth, a yawn slipped out and she had to concede that perhaps she was more tired than she thought.

*****

Everywhere they turned made Alexis more and more excited for the project. The library had been literally carved from the mountain. Ryuu pointed out great works of art as they passed pillars and walls. He explained how the original dragons had used the various elemental nano machines to help create the maze of tunnels, and as the generations passed, new dragons continued the construction until the entire mountain was one giant facility of knowledge.

Both Ryuu and Ladon described how dragons would travel from all over the universe to deposit what they had learned here. Ryuu talked of the numerous scholars and royalty that had requested information from the dragon library. He talked about the cherished handmaidens who maintained this place as well as the monastery that once house hundreds of human monk scholars.

Alexis gleaned from their conversations that dragons were often worshipped as deities, which only made sense considering their long lifespans and transformative abilities. They spoke of many positive things that occurred in their shared past. In fact, many of the various mythologies could trace their roots to the Drako presence. However, Alexis knew that there was never light without shadow. Nostalgia painted the past with rose-colored glasses; even humans did that. After all, how many people wished to 'live in simpler times'? It made Alexis wonder if the answers to what happened to the dragons lay more in the shadows of history rather than its glory.

She made a mental note to see what she could find about dragon conflicts, but first she needed something clarified.

"Both you and Ladon have referenced these

nano machines as the source of many of your magical-seeming abilities. In my world, that refers to a tiny machine."

Ladon spoke up, "It is the same for us in a way."

Alexis raised a questioning brow and waited for Ladon to continue.

"Our nano machines are created at almost the atomic level. Over the course of our world's history they developed a symbiotic relationship with our people."

Ryuu interrupted, "Our early history was lost, so no one really knows where the nano machines came from. They were obviously something created by someone, but since they are self-replicating and mostly self-sustaining, they act almost like living creatures. We do not know how to create them any longer. They just are, so to speak."

"If you can't create them then how do you get them?"

"Every person on Drako has nano machines within their body. The strength and capability of the machines correlates to the strength of the individual. We can send some of the machines out for a brief time, which allows us to glean knowledge and analyze people and things around us, but if those machines do not return to us after a certain time they shut down, essentially becoming inert dust," Ladon continued.

"Fascinating...I assume that the nano machines have something to do with your longevity?"

"Yes, they help repair vital cells and speed recovery after injury."

"If I was a biologist or an engineer I would love to get my hands on you."

Ryuu shrugged, "At your present level of technology, your scientists wouldn't find the nano machines. You are just barely delving into the world at the atomic level. Our DNA wouldn't even raise too many questions. The warriors stationed here interbred with many of the local inhabitants, so while certain traits may seem rare, they will still be present in population at large."

"I suppose that is where the myth of shapeshifters in many cultures came from."

"That I can't say." Ryuu looked thoughtful. "As far as I know, only a pureblood Drako has been able to shift. Can you shift, Alexis?"

Alexis took a step back, eyes wide, "Why on earth would you ask me that?"

Alexis's eyes darted back and forth between the two men. Ladon had suddenly become interested in the carved column next to him.

"Ladon, what did you tell Ryuu?" Alexis's eyes narrowed

14

Ladon watched Alexis as she pulled on a pair of soft white gloves. Carefully, she reached into a stack of papyrus to extract a scroll. She worked nonstop for going on ten hours. Ladon had only been able to pull her away long enough to scarf down a sandwich a few hours ago.

She had handled the discovery of having an alien ancestor surprisingly well. But Ladon was learning that nothing should surprise him about Alexis Carmichael.

Ryuu had gone off to another level of the library, leaving Alexis to sort through numerous clay barrels filled with Greek and Egyptian text. It seemed that at least for a time after Ryuu had fallen into stasis that the library continued to be used. The entire room Alexis was sorting through was deposited after his slumber, according to Ryuu.

Ladon was very aware of the fact that he was finally alone with the woman who had haunted his thoughts and dreams for the past five years. He couldn't help but stare at her. She fascinated him, and he was highly annoyed that he did not appear to have the same effect on her. She had gone about her business without a single glance in his direction.

This couldn't go on any longer or he was going to go mad.

*****

Alexis translated the same line of hieroglyphs at least six times. The hair on the back on her neck stood up and she knew that he was staring at her once again. It was disconcerting how she seemed to know exactly where in the room Ladon was. She really wished he would go somewhere else so she could do her job.

The silent watching was irritating her last

nerve.

"I would think that a race advanced enough would have at least had some sort of computerized cataloging system for this…." Alexis waved a hand in the general direction of the piles of scrolls.

She saw Ladon lip curl slightly in an upward direction. "You would have to ask Ryuu about that. He's the scholar. I was just a soldier stationed here."

"A soldier?" Alexis questioned.

Ladon straightened from the pillar he had reclined against. His eyes fixed on Alexis and he stalked forward. Alexis had the fleeting thought that he reminded her of the great jungle cats that had stalked her dig when she was an intern in the Amazon.

"To be precise, I was a hunter." Ladon advanced on Alexis as she unconsciously retreated until her back was against a wall. "And know this, Ms. Carmichael…my prey never eluded me for long. I always got my prize."

Alexis cleared her throat. "And what exactly did you hunt?"

"Every race has its fair share of a criminal element." Ladon shrugged. "With our physical strength and technology, we could not let them run amok, especially among less developed races."

Alexis put the papyrus she was working on aside and propped her chin up with one hand. She studied Ladon for a moment. If she hadn't seen him shift into a dragon for herself, she would have believed he was just a very handsome human male. It would have been easy for any of his species to blend in and take advantage of ancient Earth societies.

"Why did your people come here?"

"That is a rather complicated question." Ladon ran a hand through his short hair, causing it to stand up in disheveled spikes.

"I've got time."

Ladon hooked the toe of his boot on the leg of a nearby stool and pulled it closer. He sat down and absently traced the pattern on the leather binding of a Greek scroll in front of him. "The people of Drakos were natural-born explorers. I suppose that is a side effect of the freedom of flight. You always want to see what it beyond the next horizon. This wanderlust naturally extended to the stars. We befriended many advanced species and studied a few not so advanced."

"So Earth was a science experiment?"

Ladon laughed, "Actually it was more of a vacation resort. Earth's solar system was basically the midway point between the known universes of my time. So, the Drakos council decided to create a way station here. Surprisingly, it was discovered that we were genetically compatible with the native population, so we took an active role in the development of your society."

Alexis straightened up, stretching a back made stiff from sitting on backless stools. "I always wondered why every single culture, no matter how primitive or advance, had dragons in their mythology. I never did buy the idea of it being a genetic memory from our early evolution days when we were snack food for predators."

"We colonized this planet after you had reached the homo sapien level of evolution."

Alexis reached across the table and laid her hand over Ladon's. The contact felt like an electrical current shot up her arm. She was about to ask him if he felt it too when he pulled his hand free from hers and stood up.

As Ladon walked through the chamber door, he casually tossed over his shoulder, "I'll let you get back to work. I know you have a lot to do."

She did have a lot to get done. But having Ladon retreat while informing her of the fact hurt, and Alexis wasn't prepared to examine why just yet.

*****

Damn the man! Alexis tossed and turned, but it was no use. She couldn't sleep. She punched her pillow, briefly wishing it was Ladon's face. She groaned and buried her face in her pillow. She didn't understand him. He abandoned her and ruined her career then waltzed back into her life like nothing happened again. He ran hot and cold. Sometimes she got the feeling that he had thought about her as much over the years as she thought about him, but then he would shove her away like he hated her.

God, if it wasn't for the fact that this was the opportunity of the lifetime for a scholar, even if she couldn't publish her findings, she would just walk away. She sure didn't need the stress of dealing with a surly-assed dragon. But she couldn't fool herself…she may not need him, but she wanted him. She had never reacted to a man on such a visceral level, like she did with Ladon.

Alexis flopped on her back. Ryuu had put

her into a room that had a window that overlooked the sea. The salty breeze was cooling on her fevered skin. She turned her head to stare out at the clear, starry sky. She found constellations and recalled the myths surrounding them. She used to do that as a child when she felt overwhelmed by life. She and her father used to lay out in an open field in the bed of his truck and star gaze. It was just a hobby for a working man who barely finished high school, but those stories and the bright twinkling stars were where her love of the past first developed. So even after she had lost him to an accident at the drilling site when she had been a teen, Alexis still took comfort in stars and stories.

She rolled over, hugging her pillow as she watched the night sky. The moon was bright and full tonight. With a groan, she crawled out of bed. She wasn't going to get any sleep tonight so she might as well get up. She walked to the window and looked out over the vast sea. It made her feel small and insignificant, which in her present state just made her feel depressed.

She was meditating on the moon's reflection sparkling on the waves of the sea when a shadow passed across the sky. Alexis looked up to see a huge winged creature cross the moon's light. A dragon…Ryuu or Ladon must be out flying.

She rested her chin on her hands and watched. Despite the monstrous size, the dragon was graceful in flight. It turned and dived, skimming across the ocean waves, only to suddenly shoot into the sky with a slight adjustment of wing. It was a beautiful dance and she was the first human to see it in thousands of years.

That alone was worth the trip.

It had been two weeks, and the only one making discoveries was Alexis. She had always wondered why dragons were the only mythological creature to appear in every culture on Earth. Her colleagues argued that dragons were a genetic memory that mashed together numerous predatory features from when their ancestors were still hunted as prey. Alexis discovered that there had been numerous dragon settlements like the one she dug up in Wales all over the world. She wasn't the first archeologist to discover these places either.

"Did you know that King Tut's tomb was actually a dragon's home like yours Ladon?" Alexis didn't even look up from the manuscript she was examining when she spoke.

"Actually I did. Apep was a friend of mine. I used to visit there often."

"Apep? The Egyptian god of chaos?"

Ladon became quiet and laid down the scroll he was examining. Alexis looked up at him. He was staring off in the distance with such a lonely look that it made her heart ache.

"Did something happen to him?"

"It is an old tale…a tale the seems to play out too often in the life of a dragon."

Alexis carefully rolled the old papyrus and set it aside. She cocked her head and waited.

Ladon continued, "Our people were having difficulty surviving. When a Drakos child is born, it is almost always male. Our dragon genetics favor the masculine and often override the typical genetic markers that allows a female embryo to develop. Because of this, we were forced to search the stars for compatible breeding companions. We were encouraged to father as many children as possible to ensure the continuation of our species."

Alexis raised one eyebrow at him. "Hence the harem of handmaidens?"

Ladon shrugged. "It is the way of my people…at least it was."

Alexis winced when Ladon turned his face away from her to stare off into nothing. She hadn't meant to remind him that something dreadful had happened here on Earth to his people and that they didn't know how far the event stretched. She laid a hand on his arm.

"What happened to Apep?" Alexis asked quietly.

Ladon turned his golden-fire eyes to her. He seemed to be trying to memorize her face.

With a heavy sigh he continued, "Rarely a dragon is so drawn to one particular female that he forsakes all others. A dragon can be rather obsessive about the things they desire—one of the reasons your mythology has stories of dragon hordes. When that obsession is a person instead of things it can be dangerous because dragons can be relentless. But occasionally an event so rare occurs that it is practically in the realm of legend."

Ladon paused like he was trying to decide if he should continue. Alexis stared at him with an expectant look on her face. She could be stubbornly patient when she had to. She knew her strategy had worked when Ladon groaned and wiped his face before turning back to face her.

"A true mate…Apep had found his true mate. Not only did her feelings for him border on obsession just like his, but they both were more concerned with the other's happiness and well-being than that obsession to be together.

There was a revolt against Drakos authority in the area you now call Egypt. It was led by a human named Ra. He was resentful of the power we dragons were able to wield and was convinced that if he somehow destroyed that dragon that he could gain his power."

Alexis was transfixed by the story. She had hundreds of questions burning in her mind. How did Ra go from man to god? Why was Apep called the god of chaos? How did Tut end up making Apep's home his tomb? It was difficult to contain everything she wanted to ask; but she sensed that Ladon would reveal more if she remained quietly attentive.

"Ra attacked Apep's home with an army of

humans. Apep had sent all of his handmaidens away after he found Hathor."

"Hathor? The goddess of love?" Alexis exclaimed.

Ladon chuckled, "You know I teased Apep relentlessly for always calling her that."

"It amazes me that you lived through the creation of our world's mythology. I could write a dozen dissertations on the information I am learning here."

"You can't do that, Alexis," growled Ladon.

Alexis crossed her arms in front of her chest and glared at him. "I said I *could* not that I *would.* I'm not stupid, Ladon. I know that if our modern world found out about you and Ryuu that scientists would want to dissect you and see just how you work."

Ladon had enough sense to look chagrined. "I never said you were stupid." Why did he always seem to get Alexis's hackles up?

"Just finish the story, Ladon."

"As I was saying, Hathor was Apep's true mate. But she was also one of the main reasons Ra revolted against Apep. Hathor's family had originally agreed to a betrothal between Hathor and Ra. It would have connected the two most powerful human families in the area. But then Apep saw her and all was lost. He approached the family to have her assigned as a handmaiden in his home. They actually refused, which was rare since humans at that time considered the Drakos to be gods on earth."

"The family went against their god?" Alexis was shocked.

Ladon shrugged, "At that point Apep was considered the kindest of us all. He never forced any woman to be his handmaiden. Ra's family, on the other hand, was considered brutal to cross. It would have been suicide for Hathor's family to go against them."

"But Hathor ended up with Apep."

Ladon smiled. "Hathor was a rather forceful woman. She saw Apep when he visited her family and wanted him just as much as he wanted her. So she snuck away in the middle of the night and walked into Apep's complex as pretty as you please. When the guards tried to stop her, she announced to them that she was Apep's bride, not a handmaid to service him." Ladon laughed at the memory. "I happened to be visiting and decided to scare the upstart human, so I shifted and confronted her. She bopped me on my snout and complained about my manners…. She was magnificent."

Alexis couldn't stop the pang of jealousy Ladon's admiration for a long-dead woman caused.

"Hathor and Apep were inseparable at that point. He gave each of his handmaidens a fortune and dismissed them back to their families. He devoted his time to creating numerous works of art in her image."

"That explains why so much of Tut's treasure seemed to depict a woman instead of a male pharaoh."

"For a while the pair lived in peaceful bliss. Hathor became pregnant and they were both overjoyed, until Hathor's family came to get her."

"Why did they wait so long to try and retrieve her?"

"Honestly, they were glad that she was happy and they had a powerful alliance with the local deity."

"If that is the case, it doesn't make sense to try and take her away…." Alexis stopped and thought for a moment, then snapped her fingers.

"Ra!"

Ladon nodded. "Ra's family started a war against Hathor's because of the broken betrothal. Even with the reinforcement of Apep's human followers, Hathor's family was losing. As a last hope, they negotiated a truce, but it only went into effect if Ra had Hathor. Ra was known for his cruelty to those he considered to have betrayed him. Hathor carrying another's child would have been the ultimate betrayal, and everyone knew that Ra would most likely kill her and her unborn child."

"That's horrible. Her family was willing to sacrifice her to save their own necks."

"Which earned them Apep's wrath. Apep was a fire dragon like me, but his flame was even hotter than mine, so it usually burned blue to match his scales in dragon form. He turned her father and brothers to ash because they knowingly would send his beloved to her death."

"Talk about not getting along with your in-laws," mumbled Alexis.

Ladon smiled, but then turned serious again, "Ra used their deaths as proof that the god Apep had gone mad. He could be very charismatic when he wanted to be. Ra whipped the humans into a frenzy and convinced them that a dream prophecy had come to him that he would be the destroyer of the gods."

Alexis sat back into the chair, amazed. "Wow. I am assuming that he accomplished his goal somehow considering his role in the Egyptian pantheon. How did he manage that? You gave me the impression that your physical strength, not to mention technological strength with your nanobots, would make defeating an army a piece of cake."

"You would be correct. But Ra only used his armies as a distraction to get to his real goal."

"Hathor…."

"Yes, he kidnapped her and tried to force her to submit to him. She was heavily pregnant at this point. When she refused, he beat her until she lost the child."

"Oh my god…."

"The trauma was too much for her. Apep and I arrived shortly after. Ra had fled when he knew we were coming. We found Hathor lying there in a pool of blood clutching their dead child to her breast, weeping. The trauma had been too much for her; the nanobots in her body couldn't stem the loss of blood from her ruptured uterus. She died in

Apep's arms."

"How horrible."

"He incinerated his wife and son and spread their ashes to the wind, as is our custom."

"Your people are probably one of the reasons so many cultures preferred funeral pyres instead of burial."

Ladon nodded. "Perhaps…." He continued the sad tale. "After the loss of Hathor, Apep went mad with grief. He started to destroy all the people around him. He considered all humans his enemy because of Ra's actions. The more he rampaged, the more support Ra garnered from the surrounding people until one day Ra had created an army so large not even a Drakonian could stand against it."

"Where were you at this time?" Alexis asked. She knew Ladon well enough that she didn't think he would abandon his friend.

"I was forced to be an observer at that point. Our governing council had ordered all others on this planet to not interfere. The council was debating whether they should intervene or perhaps even destroy Apep themselves since he had become a scourge for the local population. Honestly they were relieved when Ra managed to kill Apep. After that, it was decreed that should a true mate be found, the pair was to be taken from Earth and returned to Drakos."

"They didn't want a repeat of what happened to Apep."

Ladon gave a harsh laugh, "More like they didn't want to lose the breeding opportunity on Earth. At that time, more Drakos were being born here than any other of our breeding colonies."

Alexis tapped a finger on the ancient wooden table they sat at. Something seemed off.

"If Earth was the most successful breeding program, why did the Drakos abandon it?"

"That is what we are trying to find out, Alexis."

Ladon massaged the bridge of his nose. The action brought Alexis's attention to his face. She could see the strain around his eyes. He was obviously not sleeping well, and the stress was beginning to show. Alexis got up and started to massage his shoulders. She wasn't sure why she did it, but a part of her couldn't stand to see Ladon hurting so much.

Ladon moaned in bliss. "Damn that feels good."

Alexis giggled. "You are easy to please, aren't you."

Ladon reached up and entwined his fingers with Alexis, stopping her wonderful massage. He turned his head and stared at her intently. Alexis felt like a rabbit caught in the sights of a wolf.

"I think anything you do would please me, Alexis."

Ladon's voice was pitched low and rough. It sent a shiver straight through her lady parts and she could feel the heat of a blush rising up her face. She extracted her fingers from his.

"Yeah…well…um, I've got to go do that thing that I have to do." She fled from Ladon's presence like a scared hare.

Ladon smiled at her retreating backside. So, she wasn't totally unaffected by him. That was good to know.

Alexis, Ladon and Ryuu fell into a routine over the next couple of weeks. Alexis was perfectly content to examine the numerous manuscripts housed in the dragon library. The amount of history housed there could keep her happily occupied for years. Despite her own elation at each new manuscript, she could see that the lack of information about what happened to cause them to fall into stasis was wearing on the men.

Being an archeologist, Alexis was used to

having to change the nature of her research on the fly as the dig sites yielded new items. She may not be digging in the dirt, but they were digging for information in the library's archives. It was still possible that somewhere in the thousands of manuscripts someone recorded what happened to the dragons. However, the more they dug, the more unlikely it became that they would find that specific information.

Alexis tried to talk to Ladon about shifting their focus. Unfortunately, he was as single minded in the search as he could be in business. It never pays to be inflexible when dealing with history.

They were looking through a section of the library that had been stocked by humans centuries after the dragon's stasis. Ladon had hoped that maybe some myth or legend had developed after the dragon's disappearance to point them in a direction. Alexis tried to tell him that was a waste of time because they found no reference to their disappearance in earlier manuscripts. But as usual he wouldn't listen. She slammed a leather-bound medieval manuscript, giving away just how frustrated she was.

Ryuu was the only one sitting across the work table since Ladon had left in a huff after Alexis had tried to reason with him. Ryuu raised his head and frowned at Alexis.

"Sorry," Alexis mumbled.

Ryuu carefully closed his own text and just watched Alexis. His intense gaze made her uncomfortable. She fidgeted under his scrutiny until she couldn't take it anymore.

"He just drives me crazy," Alexis exclaimed, throwing her hands up with a huff.

"I am assuming you are referring to Ladon."

Alexis crossed her arms under her breasts and glared at Ryuu. "Of course it is Ladon. No one else is on the twice forsaken rock, are they?"

Ryuu's lip twitched as he tried to suppress his amusement. He had never seen two people who got under each other's skin more than Ladon and Alexis. He wondered if they succumbed to the attraction that was simmering beneath the surface whether they would keep antagonizing daily. Probably would. Ladon was a fire dragon after all, and they were notoriously abrasive and pig-headed.

"What did he do now?" Ryuu asked.

"He completely disregards my suggestions

for this investigation," Alexis growled. She jumped up from her chair and started pacing. The energy of her anger had to go somewhere, and it wasn't fair to take it out on Ryuu. "Divining history from clues is my area of expertise. No offense, Ryuu, but I'm more knowledgeable about piecing together a narrative from bits and pieces than even you."

Ryuu inclined his head in acknowledgement. Alexis wasn't boasting and he knew it. She had a real talent for archeological work. Ryuu might be a scholar, but until he woke up in this new century he had dealt with the knowledge of the age, not ages past.

Alexis barreled on. "Ladon came to my job begging for me to come on this expedition because he needed my expertise. And now he just ignores me when I say something he doesn't want to hear."

She uncrossed her arms and flopped back into the chair across from Ryuu. One hand began to drum a nervous rhythm on the table's surface. Ryuu laid one of his large hands on top of her, stilling her fingers. She looked up at him, and he could see the tears shimmering in her eyes.

"So tell me what you have been trying to tell Ladon," Ryuu said softly. "I promise I will listen with an open mind."

"If we were going to find any references to the disappearance of dragons, we should have found some sort of clues by now."

"We have only gone through a fraction of the contents of this library," Ryuu reminded Alexis.

"I know, but there should have been some crumbs of information somewhere. We have pulled texts from all points in the history of this library. There should have been references in the later texts at least. It seems almost like someone erased that event from history. Especially at this library, you falling asleep and not being able to wake you…no other dragons visiting when this had been a hub of learning and travel according to you…. It makes no sense."

"So you think those references were purposely removed. To what end?" Ryuu asked.

"I have no fucking clue. But this feels like a systematic erasure of a major historical event. I would stake my professional reputation on the fact that no matter how much we search this library we won't find what he is wanting to find." Alexis sighed and ran her hand through her halo of dark curls.

Ryuu was thoughtful for a moment. "Okay, let's assume that you are correct. How would you proceed? Do you give up on the answers? What?"

Alexis leaned back in her chair and stared up at the beautifully painted ceiling. She couldn't see all of the detail because they were working by lantern light since the nano machines that once powered the various illumination crystals that studded the area had died off long ago.

"The best research comes in without preconceived notions." She leaned forward and looked Ryuu in the eyes while she spoke. Ryuu's respect went up; few could look a dragon, even a friendly one, in the eye without flinching.

Ryuu interjected, "Isn't it human nature to form some sort of conclusion?"

Alexis smiled, "Of course, which makes the best research nearly impossible. However, you can still be a good researcher if you keep an open mind and a flexible research path. This allows you to adjust as new information is discovered."

"But we know the event we are searching for happened, so how does the new information apply to us?"

"True, and our goal is to find the 'why' and not the 'what' of that event. Finding a specific reference to the event is about as likely as me growing wings. Think of it like a maze. We know there is an exit, but we have turned into a dead end. We can spend eternity here turning in circles and getting nowhere or we can back track and take a different path."

Ryuu nodded. "That makes sense. I assume you have an idea of what path to take next?"

"Of course."

17

"She makes sense, Ladon." Ryuu could barely hide his irritation with Ladon. For three days Ryuu had been trying to talk some sense into the stubborn fire dragon.

"What good would come from us looking for other Drakonians?" Ladon barked. "We are probably the last of our kind on this backwater planet. We need to concentrate on why we fell into stasis."

Ryuu grabbed Ladon by the shirt and shook him. "What do you think we would be doing, *baka*?"

Ladon shoved away from him, "Wasting time. Even if we find others, they wouldn't remember what happened just like you and me. And did you call me an 'idiot' in Japanese?"

"When the title fits...." Ryuu ran a hand through his dark hair and glared at his friend. "Alexis knows what she is doing."

"I never said she didn't."

"Then why don't you let her do her job and follow her lead." Ryuu sighed as he sat at a nearby table. "Alexis is bloody brilliant, and I think her approach would at the minimum find more of our people if she doesn't find out what happened in the past."

Ladon sat across from Ryuu. He refused to look at the black dragon. The silence stretched between them as Ladon glanced up at his friend. Ryuu just sat there with his arms crossed waiting for Ladon to continue. There were times Ladon despised Ryuu's patience.

Landon responded with a sigh of concession. "If we did it her way, we would get results too quickly."

Ryuu chuckled. "I have never seen you this

wrapped up in a woman. If you want her, take her. I know you have enough talent to get her body to respond until she says yes. Hell, I had to hide my favorite handmaidens each time you visited me in the past."

Ladon tilted his chair back and stared at the ceiling as he balanced on two legs. "She isn't like a handmaiden," he mumbled. "She is so much…more." Ladon let the chair fall back onto all four legs and looked Ryuu in the eyes. "I don't want to seduce her…well I do, but just not only that. Her mind is brilliant. She is fiercely loyal and kind. But she has a core of strength to rival the most formidable warrior of Drakos. I want all of it. I want her to give her entire being into my keeping." Ladon smiled. "Do you know she was able to disable my nano-machines and throw me out of her mind the very first time we met?"

Ryuu studied his friend. Ladon had always been the carefree, live-in-the-moment kind of man. He jumped from bedmate to bedmate so quickly that Ryuu doubted he could recall all their names. It was questionable that he had bothered to learn the names of all his sexual conquests. Ryuu couldn't remember a single female that Ladon actually wanted to get to know, let alone admire.

Ryuu sent a few nanomachines questing out toward Ladon. Ryuu could feel Ladon's confusion as well as the pull of desire that was bordering on obsession. He understood immediately the implications, but it seemed like Ladon was still in denial about his own feelings.

"It sounds like you may have stumbled upon a woman who could be your true mate," Ryuu casually tossed out there.

Ryuu wished he had a recording device. The myriad of emotions that crossed Ladon's face was comical.
Shock...disbelief...denial...embarrassment...and lastly resignation.

Ryuu laughed, "You don't have to look like someone kicked your puppy." He leaned forward, suddenly serious. "View this as the gift it is, Ladon. Most Drakonians spend centuries hoping for the kind of connection you feel. The majority of them go to their graves without feeling whole because they never find their true mate. Don't throw away something so wonderful."

"She doesn't even like me at the moment." Ladon laid his head on the table.

"Of course she doesn't, *baka*." Ryuu

smacked his friend on the back of the head.

Ladon's head popped up. "Ow."

"You have been a right beast to Alexis. You have made her feel like you don't respect her or her professional opinion. Much of the time you have been in her presence you have just snapped at her and belittled her talents. Of course she doesn't like you." Ryuu shook his head. "You are too used to dealing with handmaidens that jump when you snap your fingers no matter how big an ass you make of yourself. Alexis will never be that kind of woman. But if you pull your head out of your ass long enough to win her, she will be your life partner and not just a bedmate."

*****

Ladon wandered the deserted halls of the library, his conversation with Ryuu still echoing in his head. He hated to admit it, but the black dragon had a point. Alexis was probably his true mate. It would explain why she was in his thoughts every day and his dreams every night after only a single meeting. It would also explain his burning need to include her in this venture. He could reason that she was the best choice to help since she already knew about dragons, but that reasoning was thin at best. Ryuu could have easily found a few trustworthy scholars. No, Ladon had insisted that it had to be Alexis Carmichael.

He turned a corner where a faint light was coming from. His enhanced vision kept him from needing a lantern to navigate the warren-like paths of the library. Across the room, bathed in the golden glow of a lantern, was Alexis pouring over another manuscript.

Ladon stayed in the shadows just watching her. She really was the most beautiful woman he had ever seen. Her dark curls went whatever direction they chose. They couldn't be contained but were still incredibly soft—kind of like Alexis herself. She would never allow herself to be relegated to the role of simply a bedmate. She would demand that the man in her bed be as emotionally invested as she was. She would see it as her right to be their equal in all things and dismiss anyone who didn't live up to her expectations.

The little bit of time Ladon managed to be inside her mind allowed Ladon to understand that despite the high expectations Alexis would expect of her life partner, she would expect no less from herself. If she chose to love a man, it would be with a fierce loyalty laced with passion.

He smiled as Alexis seemed to discover

something that excited her. She furiously wrote several notes in her journal while going back and forth to the text in front of her. Ladon wondered if she would have the same intensity when she made love.

Alexis stopped and looked around in the surrounding darkness. She narrowed her eyes when she looked over into the shadow that concealed Ladon. Somehow she had sensed that he was there, and her eager, inquisitive face closed off and became a look of mild disapproval.

Ladon sighed. He had his work cut out for him if he was to make her his true mate. He forcibly pushed the panic down that threatened to surface at the thought that she may not want him in return. He only had the old tales to go by, but if a Drakonian male chose a true mate who then rejected him, his obsession would quickly turn into madness.

Ladon stepped into the dim circle of light. Somehow Alexis had known it was him who watched her from the shadows. For a moment, she didn't say anything. She just studied him, starting at his boots and going up. She couldn't deny that he was a fine figure of a man. Who was she kidding, both he and Ryuu should be illegal they were so perfectly made. The scholar in her wondered if the

Drakonians were the reason for human's societies male ideal, which surprisingly had changed little over the centuries.

Then she looked at his face. Ladon had a look there that she had never seen before. It made her feel like a lamb left to a wolf. His eyes were hungry. She couldn't suppress the shiver that swept through her body. It took all her willpower to turn away from that look and return to the text before her.

"What do you want?" She hadn't meant to bite at him, but she wasn't in the mood to deal with his boorish behavior, especially when her hormones were telling her to jump the man and have her way with him. She knew that Ladon wouldn't protest if she did just that, but as much as her body might want him, she refused to be just another notch on his belt of sexual conquests.

"I've come to apologize," Ladon said quietly.

Alexis's eyes snapped back to Ladon. She hadn't been expecting that. She opened and closed her mouth a few times. She wasn't sure how to respond to his apology.

"It's alright. I don't expect you to forgive me right away."

Ladon sighed and ran a hand through his hair, pulling at it out of frustration. The messy bedhead look it gave him did something to Alexis's lady parts. She was suddenly picturing him in her bed the morning after a vigorous night.

"Ryuu informed me that I was being a right ass to you," Ladon continued. "I just wanted to let you know that I am sorry about that and it wasn't your fault.... I have just been dealing with some stuff...I...um...." Ladon was at a loss. He didn't know what else to say to Alexis as she just sat there staring at him.

He raised his head and took a deep breath, trying to calm his nerves. He didn't understand why talking to Alexis made him nervous, but it did.

His head snapped back and his eyes narrowed at Alexis. He could have sworn he scented arousal from her. He had to fight the urge to inhale deeply again. If he had known that an apology would turn her on, he would have done it a long time ago. He shook his head, trying to dislodge inappropriate thoughts of him and Alexis tangled together.

He knew he could have her tonight if he pushed just a little, but he didn't want her for one night. He wanted her for a lifetime, and intuitively he knew that if he took her tonight, he would never have the lifetime and that was unacceptable.

"So, anyway, I'm sorry I took it out on you. Also, if I left you with the impression that I didn't value your professional opinion, I'm sorry." Ladon gave a boyish grin. "I can be a stubborn bastard when I set out on a path, but I should have deferred to your expertise."

Alexis was stunned. Ladon apologized, and he seemed sincere. Most of the men she had in her life would never have admitted they were wrong, let alone apologized for it. She wasn't sure how to react.

"Um…it's okay," Alexis said with a dismissive wave of her had.

"It's not okay…but thank you for accepting my apology. I will try to be less of an ass in the future." Ladon smiled.

Alexis chuckled. "I'm not holding my breath on that one."

The small laugh brought the sparkle back into Alexis's eyes. Ladon's reaction to that small thing was visceral. He backed away, suddenly needing to get out of there before he swept in and gathered her into his arms.

He nearly knocked over the bookshelf behind him, "Um...I've got to go do...something."

He retreated like a scared rabbit while Alexis's laughter followed him. Damn this courtship thing was going to be harder than he thought.

Alexis stared out of the darkened window. This had somehow become a nightly habit. Her eyes searched the night sky. Finally, a shadow streaked across the moon. It was harder to keep track of the two dragons tonight, as the sky was filling with the clouds of an oncoming storm.

Ladon and Ryuu darted in and out of the clouds in a dangerous game of tag. Lightening illuminated the sky, sending the bodies of the dragons into sharp contrast, if only for a moment.

The electricity in the atmosphere seemed to energize the males.

Alexis leaned against the window sill as the first drops of rain began to fall. She wondered if anyone on the distant surrounding islands could see the antics of Ladon and Ryuu. If they did, they probably reasoned the sight away as a trick of the light. A few of the older islanders might weave the tale into the myths of dragons already deeply ingrained in this region.

The scholar in Alexis wondered if the eastern cultures' deeply engrained dragon mythology was due to the existence of this library. Ryuu had said that during its heyday this complex was always bustling with visiting dragons and human scholars. It would an interesting study to see if she could pinpoint the development of the dragon myths in Asia. She turned over the idea in her mind. She couldn't include the Drakonians, obviously. For one, both Ladon and Ryuu had asked for their existence to remain secret. Secondly, spouting off about dragon shifters would have her laughed right out of the academic community—the truth had very nearly ruined her career once; she wouldn't let it ruin it a second time.

She turned away from the window as the

gentle rain turned into a raging storm. She hoped the men came in out of the storm, but she wasn't overly concerned. She pulled her journal out to make notes about the possibility of a study of dragon mythology. She laughed to herself. Wouldn't it be ironic if she became the foremost expert on the very thing that nearly ruined her career?

*****

Ladon let his mind wander as he and Ryuu flew back to the library through the typhoon that suddenly hit the island. The meteorological projections had said that the storm was supposed to go around their island, but as usual, the meteorologists were wrong.

Dragon bodies were extremely tough, but trying to fly through the hurricane-strength winds was a fool's errand even for them. But it did mean that for the next few nights, at the very least, there would be no night flights for him and Ryuu.

The confinement wouldn't matter much to the black dragon. He would just lose himself in the multitude of manuscripts found in the library. Ladon had been the one who needed the nightly exercise to keep his demons at bay. Without the flights to work off his frustration, Ladon worried that he wouldn't be able to keep his hands off Alexis. He growled and closed his eyes against the image of the sexy little scholar that popped into his head.

The wind chose that moment to give a huge gust as Ladon was coming in to land on the dragon platform high up on the mountain cliff. Something that hadn't happened since he was a young dragonling, Ladon lost control of his flight.

His eyes snapped open as he tried to compensate for the rapid decent. The wind gusted again and sent Ladon rolling. The best he could do was adjust his wings so he shot through the opening of the dragon platform instead of crashing against the unforgiving stone of the mountain cliff.

He crashed into Ryuu, sending them both sprawling across the large platform. Fortunately, the space had been built to accommodate a multitude of dragons landing at the same time, so the two dragons rolled to a stop before hitting the far side of the platform.

Both dragons shifted back into men. Ladon was on top of Ryuu, Ladon's head wedged firmly between Ryuu's legs.

"Thank the gods that we have the Drakonian uniform packs so our nanomachines form clothing for us as we shift," Ryuu grunted as he shoved

Ladon off him.

"Considering where my face was, I couldn't agree more." Ladon rolled over and stared up at the ceiling.

Ryuu chuckled as he stood up. "If you want my advice, brother—"

"I don't."

"Well you are going to get it anyway." Ryuu stood over Ladon and glared down at him. "Use the forced proximity that this storm will cause to your advantage. Court the bloody woman."

"I'm not sure how."

"Well figure it out before I decide to truss your wings and drop you off the damn cliff. The tension between you two can be cut with a knife." Ryuu huffed away and turned to glare at Ladon one more time just before exiting the platform, "And you are a fucking accident waiting to happen. Get your head out of your ass and do something about it before I do."

"You wouldn't dare!" Ladon growled to Ryuu's retreating back.

Ryuu flipped him off and disappeared.

Ladon lay on the dark platform lost in thought. The only light was the occasional flash of lightening. He knew that Ryuu was just trying to push his buttons, but the thought of the black dragon courting Alexis sent a chill down his spine that had nothing to do with the cold and wet stone floor he was lying on.

If Ryuu ever got serious about Alexis, Ladon was afraid that he would lose to the black dragon. Alexis already enjoyed the company of the other dragon, and they shared many of the same interests. Ladon comforted himself with the fact that he had never scented arousal from either Ryuu or Alexis, but it was a cold comfort. He knew that friendship can often turn into something more.

What did he have to offer Alexis? By human standards, he was extremely wealthy, but so was Ryuu. He could give her access to the field work that would give her back her career, but since they both owned the company, so could Ryuu. Every point in his favor the black dragon also had, as well as a few that Ladon didn't.

Ladon rolled over with a growl and punched the stone floor. For the first time in his long life, he felt inadequate. It was not a feeling he enjoyed in the least. He pushed himself off the floor and stalked towards the rooms he had chosen as his lair while here at the library. He wouldn't give up. He was a dragon after all; it wasn't in their nature to give up their treasures; and Alexis was the greatest treasure of all.

Alexis woke the next morning to a darkened room. The sun wasn't showing through the window like it normally did. For a moment, Alexis wondered if she woke in the middle of the night. A mighty clap of thunder startled her and a gust of wind rattled the windows.

Alexis hopped out of bed and closed the storm shudders on the inside of the window, just in case. She quickly lit a lantern in the darkness and used the satellite radio to check the weather reports. Evidently the island was caught in the middle of a hurricane-strength storm.

The storm didn't worry Alexis much. They were housed in the middle of a mountain after all; there wasn't a safer place to be in the storm. The darkness was a bit oppressive though. But she had worked under worse conditions.

Alexis went through her morning routine on autopilot. She tried to clip her hair out of her face, but the humidity had the curls going wild and she finally gave up. Alexis dressed in her customary dig uniform of a snug t-shirt and jeans with hiking boots. She added a jacket to ward off the dampness of the storm.

She opened the door of her rooms and nearly tripped over a tray of food that had been placed in front of it. It wasn't the normal protein bar and coffee that they normally had for breakfast, since none of them functioned well without at least half a pot of coffee in them.

She picked up the tray, and her stomach rumbled at the smell of warm oatmeal with maple syrup. Alexis wondered which one of the men left the bowl and just how they knew that oatmeal with maple syrup was one of her favorite morning treats.

She set the tray down, sat at the small table

near the window where she left the lantern, and picked up the napkin to place it in her lap. Beneath the napkin was a beautiful necklace. It was obviously handmade, but beautiful. It had a large crystal the same shade of blue as her eyes wrapped in a silver setting. Smaller stones of various shades of blue surrounded the larger one and cascaded down the side. While abstract, it brought to mind the idea of flowing water. Alexis was drawn to it immediately. She had always been partial to handcrafted jewelry, and this piece was a work of art.

Alexis put the necklace around her neck and smiled as she ate her breakfast.

After she ate, Alexis headed out the door and ran straight into a groggy Ryuu.

"Sorry." Alexis smiled up at the black dragon.

Ryuu rubbed his face, "First coffee...then talkie."

Alexis giggled. "I just wanted to say thank you for breakfast." She caressed the necklace at her throat. "And I want to thank you for the gift."

Ryuu squinted down at the necklace around

Alexis's neck. "Sorry to burst your bubble, princess, but I had nothing to do with that. Hell, I'm not even awake yet," he yawned. "Besides if I was trying to impress you, I would have sent you an ancient book of love poems. Jewelry is Ladon's specialty since his nanos have an affinity for minerals."

Ryuu waved her off as he walked towards the area they were using as a kitchen. Alexis wasn't sure how to react to the knowledge that this morning's surprise was the work of Ladon alone. She had never had a man go out of his way to do something nice for her.

A small smile played on her lips as she looked down at the beautiful necklace. Somewhere deep inside she was happy that it was Ladon who gave her such a thoughtful gift.

Alexis blushed and dropped the necklace from her hands like it burned her. Thankfully the chain was still around her neck, so it didn't fall to the floor. What was she thinking? Ladon wasn't for her. He was arrogant, rich, and ran in circles that she would never circulate in. He had ruined her career. If that wasn't enough, he wasn't even human…. He was a damn dragon for god's sake.

Good manners dictated that she needed to thank him for such a gift, but she didn't have to give him more than gratitude.

*****

The storm raged for nearly a week, and every morning Alexis woke up to some new gift. This morning it was a piece of poetry that was so bad it made her laugh. She still tried to maintain a professional distance, but Ladon was chipping away at her resolve a little bit more every day.

Alexis knew that she should probably just tell Ladon that he was wasting his time. Every time she opened her mouth to do just that, she ended up blushing and spouting off some nonsense about what she had discovered in the library. Alexis rubbed her face and sighed. Who was she kidding? She was beginning to fall for the stupid dragon like an adolescent with a crush.

She knew their species were genetically compatible. After all, that was the reason his species had come to Earth to begin with. Right now they didn't even know if there were any more Drakonians in existence. Ladon and Ryuu might be the last of their kind.

But what if they weren't? It was possible that there might be an entire civilization of dragons somewhere in the stars. If that was the case, Alexis seriously doubted that Ladon would choose her over his entire culture.

She opened the storm shutters and leaned against the window sill. The rain still poured in sheets, but the wind wasn't as severe. The storm would probably clear by tomorrow. But she wasn't seeing the rain. She was seeing the face of an arrogant dragon who had a sweet steak to him. Instinctually, Alexis knew he was dangerous to her in a way that no man had ever been before. Little by little he was stealing away pieces of her heart.

A knock at her door startled Alexis from her thoughts.

"Are you alright, Alexis?" Ryuu's muffled voice came from the other side of the door while she quickly shuttered her windows once more.

"I'm coming," Alexis called.

She knew that Ryuu was worried about her. He had become a good friend, and she saw the looks he gave when he caught her looking sad. He hadn't asked, but he knew Ladon had been courting her. In the beginning, he almost seemed to be encouraging it. But as the week progressed and Alexis became more quiet and thoughtful, Ryuu began to wonder if it was a mistake to encourage the obvious sexual tension between Alexis and Ladon.

Alexis forced a smile on her face before opening the door and breezing past Ryuu. "Let's get started. I want to get into the new chamber we discovered to see if we can find anything new."

"I think it might be best if you stop courting Alexis."

Ladon nearly fell over in his chair when his friend walked in with that announcement. He steadied himself and turned to Ryuu.

"Were you not the one who told me that I shouldn't let a woman who could be my true mate go?" Ladon's eyes shifted from his friend to the woman haloed in lantern light at the other end of the chamber. He wasn't blind. He knew why Ryuu was concerned. Something had changed in Alexis this last week. Ladon had worried that she hadn't liked his gifts, but he saw her caressing the necklace whenever she stopped to think about something. It was an unconscious gesture, but it told him that she viewed the gift as something precious to her.

Ryuu slumped in a chair next to Ladon and sighed. "I was, and I still don't think you should let her go, but something is definitely bothering her."

"I know.... I see it too."

The pair sat in silence and watched the woman they both cared for work. Ladon tore his eyes away from Alexis and studied the chamber they were in.

"Ryuu, why did you call this place the 'new chamber'?"

"Hmm? Oh...I guess because I remember we had just started construction of it before I fell into that forced stasis."

Ladon thought for a moment, "Wouldn't that mean that the humans at the very least continued to use this place after that?"

Ladon's train of thought finally hit Ryuu's

station. "Well fuck…that means everything in here would have been deposited after whatever happened to us."

"I never knew you could be slow on the uptake, Ryuu," Ladon laughed.

Ryuu punched his friend's arm and growled, "Well if I wasn't so distracted by your train wreck of a love life, I would have thought of it sooner."

"In any case, we should probably buckle down. If there are answers to be hand in this library about that time, they will most likely be here."

"Aye, aye, Captain!" Ryuu stood with a mock salute and walked away to start cataloging the various manuscripts to narrow down the ones that would most likely be the most useful.

Ladon shook his head with humor as his friend walked away. Then, like the pull of the sun on the planets, his eyes returned to Alexis. She was beautiful, but he could see the dark circles under her eyes. She hadn't been sleeping well, and it pained him to think he might be the cause. If he was an honorable dragon, he would let her go and not complicate her life. Ladon sighed. He might be an honorable warrior, but he was too selfish a man to let go of a treasure like Alexis. So somehow he had to figure out why she was troubled and do his best to fix it. That was what a good mate would do after all.

*****

"Yes!"

Ladon and Ryuu looked up from the manuscripts they were sorting to see Alexis jumping up and down and wiggling around in some sort of strange dance.

The men set their manuscripts aside and walked over to Alexis. They just stood there grinning at her until she turned to see them standing there. She stopped immediately and a deep blush creeped up her face.

Ladon laughed. "What did you find?"

Alexis cleared her throat and was once again the epitome of a professional. "When we perused the chamber in the beginning, I thought that I saw something that looked like a census record in this area and I was right."

"Every few years we recorded which Drakonians decided to settle on Earth for a while. It also helped keep track of any children that may have been born." Ladon shrugged. "Those records are thousands of years old. I don't see why you are so excited by them."

Alexis pulled her journal out. "This is just a rough translation. Eastern kanjis are not my forte, so I had to rely on what I could decipher using a modern translation dictionary. This is far from accurate, but it gave me an idea of content. Look at this line here." Alexis pointed to a line of script. "If I am right, this census was taken after y'all went into stasis."

Ryuu snatched the manuscript, causing Alexis to cringe at his rough treatment. Thankfully this document had been recorded on wooden slats instead of fragile vellum or papyrus.

His eyes scanned and widened. He could easily translate the ancient script, as he had seen it regularly in his lifetime.

Ladon recognized Ryuu's shock. "Out loud. If you don't mind," he demanded.

"The date is written as 'three years after the gods slept.'" Ryuu's eyes bored into Ladon's. "This document was a census of dragon kind taken after we were forced into stasis."

The implication of that document staggered Ladon as Ryuu continued to scan the document.

"There are more of us?"

Ryuu opened the document fully, "I believe so, but I don't know how many. This document is only one of a set, and time, vermin and the elements have damaged this one. We may not be able to fully reconstruct this document to know for certain."

"Alright gentlemen. We are going to leave the section you were working on and concentrate on this area. I have already started cataloging the manuscripts and where each was found. We will start where this particular manuscript was found and work our way out in a spiraling grid."

Alexis quickly took control in a professional manner, and for once neither man countermanded her instructions. Finding clues in the ancient past was her area of expertise after all.

"Ryuu, since you are the resident expert on ancient languages, I want you to pull and scan the documents." She handed Ladon a journal and a site map. "I've already plotted a grid for this section and did a quick sketch. As Ryuu pulls the manuscripts, I want you to assign it a catalogue number and mark on the map where it was found." Alexis picked up the manuscript that started this whole thing. "I will begin preservation on this piece. Ryuu, scan the documents and sort them by their possible usefulness. Normally, I would want to systematically work through the find, but I understand that if others are stuck in stasis like you two were that you would want to find them as soon as possible."

The trio worked in relative silence for several hours. At the end of the day approximately a dozen documents were set aside to be studied first. Each seemed to contain clues to a possible location of a 'sleeping god.' Alexis had documented each with high resolution photography but had only begun the preservation of the first one she had found. Worst case scenario they at least had the digital copies of the information. Alexis stood and stretched. She called to the men that she was going to take a break and asked if they wanted anything. Both men's stomachs decided to rumble loudly at that point. Alexis laughed and told the men that she was going to go fix them something to eat before they continued.

When she left the chamber, Ladon turned to Ryuu. "She set aside her professional curiosity to make finding our people a priority."

Ryuu glanced over to where Alexis had left the room. "She has a kind spirit…."

"I know…did you know that I read the

reviews about her on 'Rate my Professor'?"

Ryuu laughed, "Yes I know. You cyber stalked her the entire time you were apart. Let me guess, she was a tough teacher."

Ladon thought about it. "I would say most likely. The students who posted a review either loved her or hated her; but there was a common thread even with the ones who hated her class...."

"Well?" Ryuu asked.

"Even those that hated her class stated that she was always available to help them. Alexis truly cares about the people around her. She isn't like a lot of other scientists that care only about knowledge and discovery first. To her the most important things are the people, not the knowledge."

"She would have made an excellent dragon-mate queen in the past."

Ladon smiled and stood up to follow Alexis, "She will make an excellent dragon-mate in the future, and she is a queen always to me, even without the crown."

Ryuu watched his friend chase after his chosen mate with a smile that faded when he turned back to the piles of manuscripts in front of him and the chaos of Ladon's notes. The pair was more alike than either would admit; both had a habit of leaving the mess for Ryuu to clean up in the kitchen, and it appeared that was going to spill over to the research as well.

Ladon found Alexis in their makeshift kitchen. She was in front of the propane grill cooking up huge steaks for him and Ryuu. A smaller chicken breast was off to the other side, which Ladon knew was for Alexis; he had discovered she wasn't overly fond of red meat.

Ladon leaned against the door frame and observed his future mate. The fact that he remembered these small details about her was one of the things that marked her as different from past females. Ladon hadn't considered his past behavior before, but since meeting Alexis he had to acknowledge the fact that for most of his life women had been simply a tool to slate his physical needs. He wasn't interested in them beyond what he could get out of them.

It was true that he hadn't made Alexis his bedfellow yet. In his heart, Ladon knew that didn't matter. Alexis was a remarkable woman. He should know, Ryuu still gave him a hard time about his five years of obsession after only a single meeting. Ladon chuckled to himself. His instincts obviously recognized the gift that Alexis Carmichael was before his rational mind did. Ladon had wondered if his fascination would fade after spending day in and out with the woman before him. The answer was a resounding 'no!' If anything, the more time he spent in Alexis's company the more time he wanted to spend with her.

Drakonians lived a very long time compared to humans because their nano machines regularly repaired damaged cells and injuries. If Alexis agreed to be his mate, Ladon would give her an infusion of his nanos, which would eventually reprogram themselves and multiply until she had her own system of nano machines. This would greatly extend her life for centuries.

Ladon frowned as Alexis bounced around the kitchen singing to herself. If he hadn't been forced into stasis, he probably would have died before this era. Ladon rubbed his chest as he felt a visceral pain at the thought that he would never have known Alexis. It made the warrior who had always been a man of action rather than philosophy turn introspective. Maybe the clerics had been right about a greater power in the universe that guides all because he couldn't imagine a fate where he had never met Alexis. In the end, it didn't matter because she was standing there in front of him. All he had to do was reach out and grasp her.

Ladon's arm was raised and he was walking toward her when Alexis spun around at a rather exuberant part of the song she was singing. Alexis jumped with a squeak.

"Oh, I didn't know you were there." She took a couple of deep breaths to slow her racing heart. "Food should be ready in just a few minutes."

Alexis's eyes widened when she looked up into Ladon's face. She shivered at the darkly intense look she found there, but not from fear. She had often caught Ladon staring at her since he walked into her office in Ft. Worth. But she had never seen such an open look of hunger and longing before. It would be difficult for any woman with a working libido to ignore such a look. Never in her life had a look made her feel both beautiful and powerful. She knew in that instant that she was a goddess encompassing the whole of Ladon's world. It was a heady feeling.

Alexis swallowed and tried to find the words buried deep within her throat. Ladon stalked closer. He reached out and his hand trailed up Alexis's arm, leaving a burning trail of sensation. Ladon bent his head towards Alexis. He didn't ask. He didn't have to. He just took the kiss that he had been denying himself since he heard her voice on the other end of the phone line.

Ladon poured himself into the kiss and Alexis answered his call. She clung to him as he deepened the kiss. All of the uncertainty…all of the questions about the future…all of it burned away in the flames of that kiss. The past, the future…none of it mattered. Only here. Only now.

Promises were made without a single word passing between them. It was better this way. Their essence knew what they needed; thinking wasn't necessary when you were overwhelmed with feeling.

Ladon lifted Alexis in his arms. He wanted her there always, clinging to him as if her life depended upon it. He knew that he was irrevocably ensnared by her feminine power, but that prison made him feel free for the first time in his life.

"What is on fire?!" Ryuu bust through the kitchen doorway. He ran to the grill and searched franticly for the fire extinguisher.

The action was enough to raise Alexis from her lust-induced haze. She looked around, surprised to see the whole kitchen area filled with black smoke. She tried to wriggle out of Ladon's arms, but he tightened his grip.

"Ladon!"

Her alarmed cry was like a bucket of cold water on Ladon's lust. Soon everyone was searching for the fire extinguisher. Alexis had turned off the propane to the grill, but the food was consumed in flames and it flared when it hit the gas trapped in the lines.

Ladon threw open the windows and partially transformed. He used his wings to fan the smoke, pushing it through the windows to clear the air as everyone coughed. The fire finally burned itself out, but their dinner was reduced to charcoal.

Ryuu pointed a soot-stained finger at Ladon and Alexis. "The two of you are not allowed in the kitchen alone ever again."

All color drained from Alexis's face before it turned bright red. She slapped her hands over her mouth, spun on her heels, and bolted out of the kitchen before Ladon could even reach for her.

Ladon groaned and wiped a hand down his face, causing the soot to streak in lines. He looked like he was about to launch a jungle sneak attack.

"Damn it! I'm never going to get her out of her room again."

Ryuu laughed, "Well you can't say that she isn't affected by you anymore. The fire I saw in here wasn't just from the remains of dinner."

"Yeah," Ladon smiled as he turned and walked away with a whistle. Today's disaster left him oddly cheerful.

Ryuu looked around the destroyed kitchen and sighed. "I am hiring a damn maid when we get back to civilization."

22

"Alexis," Ladon called from the other side of the door.

She knew he was going to come for her, but Alexis had hoped that he would wait long enough for her to get her composure back. What had happened in the kitchen…she knew that there was a spark of attraction between the two of them, but that was a raging inferno.

Alexis could still feel his hands on her. She touched her swollen lips. No man had ever kissed her like he wanted to consume her. It was a soul-shaking experience that ruined her for any other man. Alexis was experienced enough to know that kind of passion was a rare find.

Everything in her was telling her to open the door and finish what they had started in the kitchen. Everything except fear. Fear was telling her that Ladon would possess more than her body if she gave in.

Her inner debate about whether or not to open the door was still raging as Ladon's knocks became more insistent. His temper was flaring because of her lack of response.

"Alexis, you are going to talk to me whether you want to or not," Ladon growled. His fist left a dent in the wooden door. Still she didn't answer him.

Alexis was being a coward and she knew it. Never in her life had a man knocked her so off balance. *But he's not a man. He is an alien that can turn into a fucking dragon.* Maybe that was the problem; if he had been human she would have latched onto him and done her damnedest to keep him.

Crash! Alexis's door flew open and she saw

Ladon silhouetted in the hall light, his boot still raised in the air.

Alexis knew that his violent entrance should have frightened her, but the sight of his masculine form as he stalked towards her had her shivering for an entirely different reason. Somehow she knew on an instinctual level that Ladon would never hurt her. But he would make demands of her body and possibly her heart and not take no for an answer.

Alexis gave in to the inevitable. She reached her hand out and cupped his rough cheek. Her eyes questioned as her thumb caressed his lips. Ladon's eyes closed with a moan as his face pushed into her palm as if it craved the contact. She lifted her other hand to pull him down.

Ladon's eyes opened and the golden depths seemed to burn with an inner fire. The heat between them wasn't one sided. When Alexis considered the possibility that she could demand as much from Ladon as he demanded from her, suddenly the idea of him being a different species seemed to fade into the background of her mind. It was simple: he was a male; she was a female.

Alexis nipped at Ladon's chin and smiled as the flames in his eyes flared with her touch. Her hand trailed down his neck to his chest. Her fingers traced the hard muscles beneath his shirt. Her decision was made. No more denying what was between them.

Alexis heard the voice in the back of her mind tell her that this wouldn't last, but she firmly shut it away. She was going to explore what was between her and the dragon. If it ultimately fizzled she knew that these moments would be memories burned into her psyche forever. But the future was only speculation, only now was real. And she was going to fill the now with as much sensation as she could.

Her lips found his, and like a switch his arms wrapped around her, crushing her to him. In that moment, Alexis felt something within herself break, the pieces falling reforming into something new, something that carried parts of Ladon with her. She knew that indefinable something would be with her always, even if things between them were to fall apart. Somehow she knew that today she was changed forever.

Alexis fisted her hands in his shirt and pulled him closer. Her mouth crushed his. It was a fight for dominance and both refused to surrender. As Ladon's hands trailed down her back and cupped her hips, she admitted to herself that this was what she had been searching for. She needed masculine balance, a partner, an equal. She would never have to worry about being too much for Ladon. Too intelligent, too strong, too sexual….in the past she had heard all of those from her failed attempts at finding a life partner. But Ladon would never accuse her of being too much; she was made to be his match in every facet as he was hers.

Then Ladon kissed her back and she lost every coherent thought, save one. *I want this man.*

Alexis smiled her mysterious female smile, causing Ladon to stop and look down into her eyes. She gazed up at him longingly, communicating without words. Whatever he saw there must have satisfied the questions she saw in his eyes. Because he trailed kisses across her face and neck.

Nipping at her ear, he whispered, his warm breath tickling across her skin. "I need to hear you, love. Tell me that you want this…need me the way I need you."

Alexis could hear the vulnerability in his voice. If she had any reservations left, they flew away at that sound. Her fear and longing were not one sided, and somehow that gave her strength to banish those things from her thoughts.

Alexis turned her head and captured his lips. "Yes."

Yes...that one simple word shifted Ladon's entire universe. Alexis had given herself into his keeping. Ladon knew that she didn't fully understand what she had just agreed to. This was no tumble for him; this was a lifetime. Every scale in his body knew that this was forever. Once he tasted Alexis he knew that a lifetime would never be enough. He had time. He could convince her of forever.

Alexis bit his ear with a growl to bring his

mind back to the present. The future could figure itself out. Right now he had a dragoness to satisfy.

Alexis turned and headed to the window, unbuttoning her shirt with each step. She shrugged out of her shirt and Ladon's breath caught in his lungs. Shirt fluttered to the ground leaving behind an expanse of creamy white skin. No bra...she wore no bra and her rosy nipples proudly thrust forward, beckoning Ladon to come forward and taste them. Ladon could see a drop of perspiration trail its way down between the valley of her breasts. He was so mesmerized that it took a while for his brain to register that Alexis had given him a husky laugh and crooked her finger at him.

Ladon's body tightened even more at the sound. Never had he had such a visceral reaction to a woman. No wonder Drakonians who found their true mates would forsake all others. Every experience he ever had paled in comparison to this one woman—and he hadn't even touched her yet.

Her hands reached up and fluffed her dark curls. A feline grace stretched her body as she arched her back in the moonlight. She cocked one jean-clad hip in challenge, and Ladon's dragon raked his insides trying to get to the surface.

Alexis must have seen the dragon in his eyes

as he stalked closer because her breath hitched and she raised one hand to touch his scruffy cheek.

"I don't think I have it in me to be gentle, Alexis," Ladon declared as he kissed down her throat.

"Who said I wanted gentle?"

Ladon buried his face at the juncture of her neck and shoulder with a groan. He couldn't help but inhale the tantalizing musky scent that was Alexis. He was fairly certain he would be able to track her by scent alone.

Her fragrance was ripe and feminine and laced with arousal. A growl crawled up Ladon's throat as his dragon demanded freedom. Never in his long existence had Ladon had difficulty controlling his beastly nature. It wasn't the sex; it was all Alexis. Something in that woman called to everything in him; the good, the bad, the dangerous.

Ladon lifted Alexis by her thighs, wrapping her legs around his waist, so he could bury his face between the gorgeous breasts that had enthralled him so. He suckled and licked like she was his favorite dessert. Her skin tasted like heaven. From this point on, this would be home for Ladon.

Alexis threw her head back, moving her body, hot with need, against the solid evidence of his arousal. She was hot, her entire body heated with lust.

Ladon bit down on her sensitive nipple. He felt Alexis shudder and the front of her jeans became wet.

*****

Dear god! The man was lethal. Even when she had been a hormone-crazed teenager, she had never orgasmed dry humping her partner. But Ladon seemed to be able to play her body like a master musician.

She untwined her legs from Ladon and stepped back with a hand on his chest. She could see the question and worry in his eyes. Alexis knew he was afraid that he had done something wrong. Her heart melted even more at that. Never had a lover been concerned about her comfort or pleasure before.

Alexis smiled like a Cheshire cat and shoved. She knew that with his incredible strength she would never have moved him if she hadn't caught him off guard. He took a step back, his knees buckling as he hit the edge of the bed.

He flopped on the bed and then raised himself up so he could watch Alexis. Alexis saw his eyes flash like a cat's, changing between the slitted pupil of the dragon and the rounded pupil of the man. It made Alexis hesitate.

Ladon just watched her, his dragon eyes staring at her. She wanted the man, but could she accept the dragon?

Ladon's face remained stoic, but his dragon eyes suddenly looked forlorn and lonely. That look made Alexis's chest hurt; her heart ached so bad. In that moment, she realized that the man and the dragon were one in the same and she wanted them both.

She stalked towards the bed, adding an extra sensual roll to her hips. Ladon's eyes lost their desolation as the dragon's fire returned to heat his gaze. She stood above him as he lay like a pasha across her bed. The fire in his eyes flared with each move she made. When she reached for the button of her jeans and slowly stripped them off, she was almost surprised that the linens didn't catch fire from the heat in his gaze.

Ladon attempted to reach out and grab her, but Alexis danced away, wagging a finger at him with a glint in her eye. No words were exchanged, but Ladon seemed to understand that she needed him to submit to her as much as he needed her to submit to him. He returned to watching her as he leaned back, propped up by his arms.

Alexis watched him as she crawled up his body. She could feel the heat pouring off Ladon and goose bumps race across her skin as her sensitive nipples brushed across the light dusting of hair on his chest.

She captured his mouth in a soul-searing kiss. She poured all the confusion, lust, and love she felt into that kiss, trading a bit of her soul with his. Neither one noticed the brief glow of nano machines flaring to life.

Alexis's hands trailed down his body, followed by her lips. Every few inches she would nip him with her teeth and scratch his skin with her nails. She rubbed her body across his like a cat in heat. Every other man would start complaining at her aggressiveness or that she was too rough at this point, but not Ladon. He seemed to revel in the marks she left across his skin. He closed his eyes and groaned, his body arching, begging for more. This man was made for her.

She got to his jeans and growled in frustration as the snug fit she admired from afar impeded her skin-to-skin contact. Ladon chuckled but raised his hips enough that she could pull his jeans off of him.

Finally, he was as bare as she was. She hummed her appreciation as his manhood stood demanding attention. She rubbed her body across his, marking him with her scent. Humans may not notice any difference, but Drakonians would immediately recognize her mark.

She moved up his body, until she reached his shoulder and her kisses and licks turned into a love bite. Ladon's blood surged, making his already engorged cock rock hard.

Alexis broke the skin with her bite and suckled, tasting blood. Ladon's nano machines converged on the area, not to repair the damage—to flow into the small amount of blood Alexis ingested.

Ladon's body chemistry had already changed slightly in the presence of his true mate. His nano machines tuned themselves to Alexis for this moment. Without conscious thought, Alexis began a mating ritual that predated even humanity. Those few machines began to change Alexis's chemistry immediately. She felt it as an intense heat that flushed through her body, making her lust spike.

She started back down his body, her hand reaching for his member, demanding attention.

Ladon hissed in a breath as her delicate hand squeezed him with surprising strength. Alexis could feel his eyes on her as she licked her lips. One corner quirked up as she felt, more than heard, him groan. She loved that she could affect him so much.

Hands braced on his thighs, she lowered her head, until her nose was level with the part of him she desired to taste. She closed her eyes and inhaled his masculine scent. He smelled spicy with a hint of cinnamon. She nuzzled him before licking him from root to tip. Her tongue swirled at his flared head and his hips jumped, begging for more.

She obliged him, wrapping her lips around his throbbing shaft. Her tongue felt every heartbeat through his heavily veined member. It beat a rapid tattoo as she sucked. One hand milked his base in time with the movement of her mouth and tongue. The other massaged his heavy ball sack.

Alexis lightly scraped her teeth across the sensitive bundle of nerves on the underside of his cock's head. She smiled and hummed as he fisted the sheets of the bed with a moan. She knew he was close because she could feel his balls tighten.

Suddenly she was lifted away from her new favorite toy, and Ladon's mouth crushed hers with a growl. He grabbed a handful of Alexis's hair and pulled. The small bite of pain added to the heady mix.

Ladon used her hair to direct her where he wanted her without a word. Alexis found herself on all fours at the edge of the mattress. The other hand caressed her shoulders, fingers tailing down her back as if he was trying to memorize every curve. Those fingers traced over her rounded backside. Alexis whimpered when his touch left her, only to gasp when the flat of his palm landed across her ass. The sting sent heat straight to her core and her anticipation dripped down her legs.

She arched her back, pushing her ass against his thighs; silently begging for more. Ladon pulled her hair until her head looked over her shoulder. He leaned down and captured her mouth; their tongues fighting for dominance.

In a single hard thrust, Ladon filled her; capturing her moans with his kiss. He broke away from her mouth to set a brutal pace with each thrust. It was all Alexis could do but to hold on and feel.

Every lover had taken one look at her petite frame and thought her fragile. They treated her like art glass—only to be handled with a gentle touch. She didn't want gentle. She didn't need gentle. She needed a man who would throw her down and fuck her senseless. She wanted to feel the experience days after the fact. She needed a man whose libido and fire raged just as much as hers. Hallelujah, she finally found him in Ladon.

Alexis could feel the waves of her climax rising. She pushed back against Ladon's thrusts. The sound of flesh against flesh filled the bed chamber. His thrusts were so forceful that his testicles hit her clit each time. But it wasn't quite enough to send her over the edge until Ladon reached around with one hand and started stimulating her. First he kneaded breasts and pinched her nipples, sending little electric shocks through her body. She moaned as her body melted into the sensation.

Then he pinched her clit and she screamed as the wave of her orgasm crested. Ladon increased the speed and force of his thrusts, which kept the shockwaves of her orgasm going. With a final thrust and roar, Ladon emptied himself inside her and bit her shoulder at the base of her neck, locking her in place with instincts as old as time.

His teeth broke the skin and he held her there

as her channel spasmed against his still hard member. Nano machines poured into Alexis's body from his. All the while her body milked him of everything he had until they both collapsed.

Ladon reluctantly pulled free of his true mate and rolled to the side, so as not to crush her. He gathered Alexis in his arms, her head laying on his chest. He looked down to tell her all the things in his heart, only to discover his true mate snored.

Alexis had fallen asleep almost immediately. Ladon chuckled and pulled the covers over both of them. Tomorrow would be soon enough to figure everything out.

Ladon woke to the feel of Alexis stirring in his arms. He opened his eyes when her warmth left his body. For some reason, the chill wasn't just from the lack of body heat. Ladon quietly propped himself up on one elbow and watched Alexis dress. By the stars, she was a beautiful woman, who at this moment seemed to be running scared.

"Good morning, Alexis." Ladon watched Alexis jump at the sound of his voice, confirming that she was trying to sneak out without waking him.

"Um, morning…."

"We need to talk about last night, Alexis."

"I seem to remember that we communicated quite well without talking." Alexis gave a nervous giggle.

"Alexis…."

"It's okay, Ladon. I'm a modern girl. Last night was fun, but I don't expect anything from it." Ladon tried to speak but Alexis just barreled on. "I know your first priority is to find out what happened to you and your people. Besides, we are entirely different species." Alexis pulled her jeans on and started tucking in her shirt as she gave her little speech. "We both have physical needs, and I am sure we can scratch that itch while we are thrown together. Afterwards we can part as friends."

Alexis flashed him a brilliant smile as she finished dressing. "It was just sex, nothing more."

Ladon lay in bed dumbfounded. Just sex? She thought that last night, the most meaningful night in his entire existence, was just sex. Alexis breezed out the door before Ladon could collect himself enough to call after her.

*****

Ryuu held out a cup of coffee to Ladon as he stumbled into the makeshift kitchen.

"After the noise the two of you made last night, I didn't expect to see you for at least a couple of days." Ryuu grinned as his friend glared daggers at him. "Alexis ran in here like a demon was after her and grabbed a mug of coffee and disappeared to go over my translations."

Ladon grumbled incoherently and took the mug. Something was definitely off with the pair this morning.

"I could smell the changes in Alexis's body chemistry. I take it the mating went well."

Ladon slammed the mug on the table. "According to her it was just sex," he practically shouted. He let go of the mug and buried his face in his hands with a groan. "I never wanted to tie myself to one female in all of my existence, and when I finally find the one, she tells me it was just sex."

Ryuu took a sip of his own coffee and tried unsuccessfully to curb the grin of amusement. "How does it feel now that the shoe is on the other foot?"

"Huh?"

"Do you even realize how much time I had to

spend consoling heartbroken handmaidens who thought they were special to you only to have you drop them as soon as someone else caught your interest?"

Ladon waved a hand dismissively, "The handmaidens knew that we could couple with any of them that consented."

"That doesn't mean that their emotions didn't get involved. Doesn't feel so good when the object of your affection says they don't want you, does it?"

Ladon sighed, "Okay, I get your point. I was a man-whore and this is karma."

Ryuu chuckled, "Well they say that self-awareness is the first step in growth." He set his coffee mug aside. "Seriously, I don't think you have to worry too much. The mating wouldn't have taken if her brain chemistry hadn't been primed for it, and you and I both know that requires more than a surface lust. She has to have a strong lasting emotional connection to you to produce the correct cocktail of chemicals to activate the nano machines. I could smell changes in her chemistry caused by the nano machines, so something had to be there."

Ladon perked up. "You're right. So all I have to do is convince Alexis to admit her real feelings."

Ryuu barked a laugh. "Good luck with that one. She can be as stubborn as any fire dragon." Ryuu fell silent for a moment and then continued in a serious tone, "Did you at least tell her about the nano transfer?"

Ladon looked sheepish. "I had planned on telling her this morning but she rushed out before we could talk."

Ryuu's eyes snapped to Ladon's with a glare and he reached over and smacked the back of his head. "You idiot! You are supposed to talk to them beforehand and give them a choice. You can't make a decision that changes their entire life for them."

"I know," Ladon groaned. "I just got caught up in the moment."

"That's no excuse. You have made her practically immortal in the eyes of humanity. She must learn to change her identity on a regular basis, fake aging, watch friends and family die," Ryuu's voice raised in pitch as he laid out just what Ladon had done.

Ladon ran his hand through his hair, "Look, I get it, Ryuu. I fucked up royally." He sighed deeply.

"But I can't say that I am sorry. A world without Alexis is one that I don't ever want to be in. So even if I could take it back, I don't think I would. We'll just have to figure out how to move forward from here."

Ryuu shook his head, "What's done is done; but you are going to have a long road ahead of you. Especially once she figures out that you took her choice away. Please tell me you at least warned her about the nano assimilation…"

"Uh…."

"Ladon!"

"It's alright. It usually takes at least twenty-four hours before it kicks in. I'll tell her today."

Both men turned toward the door as Alexis's cries of pain echoed down the hall. They jumped up, knocking their chairs over to rush to her aide.

25

Alexis was leafing through Ryuu's translation notes. He was a meticulous scholar. She smiled to see he even noted where certain words could have multiple interpretations. She was sitting at the work station with the documents Ryuu claimed would most likely be the greatest help. As she read through his translations, she made notes about place names and their linguistic morphology as well as the wording surrounding those reports. If she can trace the language dialect back then she could possibly narrow down the location.

She was comparing an entry whose language reminded her of the Kievan Rus' people when her entire body seized. The pain was so intense that she fell out of her chair and screamed.

Alexis felt like she was dying. She tried to crawl to the door; she needed help. But her progress was hampered by the waves of pain that caused her entire body to lock up. She whimpered as the pain receded just enough to allow her to scoot forward a minute amount before the next wave hit.

All she could do was curl herself into a ball of pain. She, who hated to cry in front of anyone, was sobbing when the men burst through the door.

Ladon was immediately by her side. He reached out to pick her up. She screamed when he touched her.

Tears flowed down Ladon's face as he blubbered, "I'm sorry. I'm sorry," over and over again.

Alexis wasn't sure what he was sorry about, but despite her own pain she tried to reach up and comfort Ladon. Her fingers just brushed at the tears on his face when molten fire flashed through her body.

Ryuu pushed Ladon out of the way and scooped Alexis up, even though she screamed once again in pain.

"Bear with it, little one. We need to get you off the floor and into a bed so we can care for you." Ryuu quickly stalked back to the sleeping areas, leaving Ladon to scramble to keep up.

He gently laid her on the bed as she clawed at the clothes on her. Even the familiar material of her shirt and jeans hurt.

"Ladon, get her clothes off of her and cover her with a soft blanket." Ryuu turned to leave. "I'm going to get some cool water and wash cloths to bathe her body. Her body is running a dangerously high fever. If we don't get that under control we could lose her."

Ladon turned and removed Alexis's shirt, shoes and socks. She cried out every time he shifted her. He had done this to her and she didn't even know it. She would never forgive him if she found out what he so callously put her through because of his own selfish nature.

He tried to remove her form-fitting jeans, but she screamed as he tried to pull them down. He searched her room for scissors to cut them from her, but he couldn't find anything. He growled in frustration as Alexis whimpered on the bed, clawing at her remaining clothes. In desperation, he called his dragon to the surface and willed a partial shift. He used his razor-sharp claws to cut away the offending material.

He had just covered the exhausted Alexis with the softest blanket he could find when Ryuu returned. The black dragon laid a hand against her skin and frowned.

"Her fever is worse. We must get her temperature down. The human brain can be damaged if the body temperature is too high for prolonged periods of time." Ryuu was all business as he dampened a cloth in water filled with ice and ran the cloth across Alexis's skin.

Alexis's eyes closed as her body shivered from the cold cloth.

"Why is she so tired?" Ladon's voice broke with worry.

"Every muscle in her body repeatedly contracted. A few minutes of that will make her feel like she has run a marathon. We are just lucky that it doesn't seem to have snapped any bones," Ryuu said matter of factly.

"Does that happen often?"

"It happened enough. Which is why consent is so important. Forcing this on someone is cruel," Ryuu bit out at Ladon.

Ladon winced but didn't argue. He knew that Alexis's pain was all his own fault. He should have talked to her before a complete mating.

"How long will this last?"

Ryuu sighed, "I honestly don't know. I've never known a human woman to succumb this quickly to the conversion. This is new territory for me."

Ladon laid a gentle hand on the sleeping Alexis only to have her pull away with a look of pain on her sleeping face.

"All we can do is keep watch and pray. If we can keep her body temperature down I think she will make it through without any permanent damage. But one of the other of us will have to stay with her. As soon as her fever spikes we have to cool her back down."

"I'll take the first watch." Ladon pulled a chair next to the bed. He grabbed a cloth and dipped it into the chilled water and almost reverently bathed

Alexis's exposed skin.

Ryuu turned to leave her room. He would work on the census scrolls for a bit, then come and relieve Ladon. He reached to close the door only to realize that it was broken, hanging only by a single hinge. Oh, well. They would be in and out caring for Alexis, so closing the door wasn't a major priority at the moment. With that he walked out.

*****

Ladon shuffled into the kitchen. Alexis's fever had subsided enough that they weren't having to maintain a constant vigil, but even so Ladon rarely left her side. Ryuu was beginning to worry about his friend. Ladon could pack everything but the kitchen sink in the bags under his eyes.

Ryuu worried about Alexis as well. He had been able to start an I.V. to keep her hydrated from the emergency medical supplies he had thankfully insisted they bring. But they had no way of feeding her while unconscious. The best they had been able to accomplish was to dribble broth down her throat. Even Ladon had quit eating, and Ryuu watched as both of his friends were fading before his eyes.

"It's been nearly two weeks, Ryuu." Ladon plopped into a chair next to the black dragon. "I may not have paid attention to the mating information for this planet, but I don't think this is normal."

Ryuu ran a hand through his now shaggy hair. "No this is not what we were informed would happen. She should have recovered by now or died."

Ladon glared at Ryuu and growled.

Ryuu raised a hand, "I'm not saying I want her to die, but this half-life in between wasn't something they briefed us about." Ryuu looked out the window to the rising dawn. For once the scholar wasn't sure what the next move should be. All his vast knowledge and the resources of the ancient library hadn't yielded an answer. All he could do was beg the universe to please spare his beloved friends.

"Our information about humanity dates back almost to their pre-history. Thousands of years have past. It is possible that something new has evolved in the population."

Ryuu's eyes widened. "Or something old has re-emerged!" Ryuu jumped from his seat and rushed into the deepest bowels of the library complex.

Ladon was too tired to follow his friend. If he found any information he would come and find him anyway. He laid his head on the table and watched as the day came to life once more. The sun rose, the birds started to chatter. Everything continued on while the woman he loved lay ill and possibly dying. If she didn't wake enough at least to start eating again, it would only be a matter of time before she faded away. Ladon rolled his head to the other side so he could stare at the stone walls instead of the rising sun. It all seemed so unfair that the world could go on like nothing had happened when his entire existence was tied to the unconscious woman down the hall.

Ladon sighed and gulped down the sob that tried to escape. For the first time in his life, he just wanted to break down, but he refused to allow himself to do so. This whole thing was his fault. He shouldn't have completed the true mate ceremony without her consent. Maybe this was the universe's punishment for his selfish arrogance. Ladon could accept that. What he couldn't accept was the suffering Alexis was enduring for his arrogance. It was a powerful lesson that Ladon had taken to heart.

Ladon forced himself to stand with a groan. He stretched his stiff muscles. Ladon knew he should eat something, but he didn't have an appetite. Ryuu had repeatedly reminded him that he would be useless to Alexis if he collapsed from hunger. So

Ladon trudged over to the cooler. A slice of ham and an apple was about all he could manage.

He had just taken a bite of the apple when Alexis's scream echoed down the hall. The apple fell from numb fingers as terror seized Ladon's heart. Then he somehow found himself sprinting down the hall, yelling for Ryuu to follow.

Ladon burst through the doorway of Alexis's bedroom to see her entire body arched off the bed, contorted in pain. He ran over, catching her just as she convulsed and nearly fell off the bed.

Ryuu found Ladon on the bed with Alexis in his arms sobbing. Never had he seen the fire dragon cry, and that shook the black dragon more than anything else. He somehow knew that should the worst happen that he wouldn't just lose Alexis but Ladon as well.

"Something's wrong. She was screaming and…." Another wave of convulsions cut Ladon off as Alexis contorted. The eyes that had been closed for so long snapped open, pupils dilated in pain. Her body twisted and contorted with such strength that Ladon was having difficulty keeping her on the bed.

Ryuu nodded and rubbed his chin as he studied the scene. "This is good."

"Good?!" Ladon practically shouted. "She is in pain."

Ryuu moved to the bed and helped Ladon secure the thrashing body of Alexis. "It's good because it means that the nano integration of her body is finally complete. They are in the final stage, adapting her neural net."

"Why is it so difficult for her?"

"All true change hurts and is dangerous, Ladon." Ryuu massaged Alexis's muscles when her body relaxed. He motioned for Ladon to do the same. She would be sore regardless when she fully returned to them, but they could ease the discomfort somewhat.

"I'm not in the mood for your philosophical bullshit, Ryuu," Ladon growled as his hands worked on the other side of Alexis. Growls seemed to be his only form of communication lately.

"It's not bullshit. Alexis is becoming an entirely different species. It is naïve to think that process wouldn't be a difficult one."

Ladon massaged the bridge of his nose. His head was killing him, but it was a minor pain compared to Alexis. "I'm sorry, friend. This whole thing is my fault. I have no right to take it out on you."

Ryuu just shrugged. "We are both worried."

Alexis's body fully relaxed and the men breathed a sigh of relief. Ryuu stood.

"I need to return to my research. There are a few things I want to verify. Don't leave Alexis alone. The next 24 hours will be critical. She will either wake up fully Drakonian or she will pass on to the next world."

"Don't sugar coat it," Ladon grumbled.

Ryuu walked over to his friend and squeezed his shoulder. "Alexis is a survivor. I'm confident that she will make it through this."

Ryuu walked out of the room, leaving Ladon alone with his beloved. Ladon picked up Alexis's hand and caressed her palm with his thumb. He brought the hand to his lips and kissed her fingers one by one.

"You've got to live for me, beautiful. I don't think I can make it without you anymore." Ladon brushed a damp lock of hair from her forehead and traced her cheek with his fingers. "You probably won't remember any of this and I should have told you what was in my heart a long time ago, but I was a coward." Ladon laid his head on the bed and watched Alexis breath. "I love you so much. You probably won't believe me, but you have become more important that even the mystery of my past. Nothing matters if you aren't in this universe to share it with me. So I'm begging you, don't leave me."

Ladon fell asleep with his fingers entwined with Alexis's.

When Ladon woke up, night had descended once again. He sat up and stretched. His stiff muscles told him that he hadn't moved for many hours. He could hear Alexis's even breathing. He was thankful that she hadn't had any more seizures. Ladon whispered a prayer into the universe that the worst was over. He reached out and brushed the curls from his woman's face. Even in sickness her hair had a mind of its own and refused to be tamed.

"Wake up, beautiful. I need to see those pretty blue eyes of yours," Ladon whispered. "I know this whole mess is my fault. I swear I didn't know it would be this bad; but that doesn't excuse my selfishness."

Alexis stirred in her sleep and Ladon continued to talk to her.

"You are the toughest woman I know. There is no way you would let a man's stupidity weigh you down for long. I need you to wake up and berate me like you normally do. You can't let the illness I caused keep you from keeping me in line. Without you I have no one to tell me when I am being an ass."

"You're always an ass...."

The sound was so quiet that Ladon almost dismissed it as wishful thinking. He looked down to find the most beautiful pair of blue eyes staring back at him.

"You look like shit," Alexis croaked with her dry throat.

Tears spilled down Ladon's cheek and he grabbed Alexis and held on like he was afraid she would disappear.

"Can't breathe..."

Ladon released her with a sheepish look.

"What is that stench?" Alexis sniffed the air. "Is that you? I mean you do look like you haven't showered in a couple of days."

For the first time in weeks Ladon laughed. Alexis wrinkled her nose and raised a weak arm and inhaled.

"Nope...that is me. Why am I so weak and why do I stink?"

Ladon smiled and caressed her cheek. "Bath first...then..." he heaved a dramatic sigh, "then we will talk."

Ladon left the room and quickly returned with a warm pot of water and a wash cloth. He carefully lifted Alexis up to change the sheets; she had remained naked during her entire illness since they never knew when her fever would spike.

Gently, Ladon bathed away the grime of illness from lexis's body. She sighed in pleasure as he massaged shampoo into her hair. All the while he explained with a neutral voice about the mating and nano machines.

As he rinsed away the last of the soap, Alexis finally spoke up, "So you are telling me that you infected me with some alien cooties which nearly killed me and now I have tiny little machines zooming around my body which have turned me into an alien myself?"

Ladon nodded.

"And you didn't think that the possibility of death as a consequence of having sex with you wasn't important enough to mention beforehand?"

Alexis was propped up against pillows, naked with only a blanket covering her, and yet, she somehow managed to convey royal displeasure at the actions of a peasant.

"I told him he was an idiot," Ryuu stated as he walked into the room. He went over to the bed and kissed Alexis's temple. "I'm so glad to see you coherent again, my dear."

Alexis smiled at Ryuu. "Thanks."

"Don't be too hard on Ladon." Ryuu smiled back as he sat next to the bed. "He's been very repentant and hasn't left your side for more than a few minutes at a time. How much do you remember?"

"I was suddenly in excruciating pain and then not much after that except for some really twisted and vivid dreams." Alexis wasn't ready to discuss the images seared in her mind just yet. "How long was I ill?"

"A little over two weeks," Ladon said. "If you hadn't woken up soon I would have called for an emergency evac to get you to a medical facility."

"If I was so ill, why didn't you?" Alexis bit at him.

Ryuu reached out and laid his hand on her arm. "He wanted to, Alexis. I wouldn't let him."

"Why?"

Ryuu sighed, "You are one of us now, Alexis. What do you think would happen if the doctors discovered the differences in your physiology? Or worse discovered that your body carried millions of tiny machines beyond the technology of earth?"

Alexis closed her eyes. She wasn't quite ready to forgive them, but she understood. If they had taken her to a hospital she would have ended up as a science experiment, most likely against her will by order of the government. The excuse of national security could cover a multitude of sins.

"So what do I do if I break a bone or contract

some tropical disease now? It's not like my field work isn't without hazards."

Ladon shrugged, "One of the perks of the nano machines is they will repair most injuries and illnesses. They will also constantly renew your body's cellular structures."

"So I'm immortal now?" Alexis grinned for the first time since this conversation started. "That's so cool."

Ryuu and Ladon chuckled.

"Not immortal, but your aging has slowed dramatically. You might appear immortal to those around you, so care must be taken with us living among humans. And you can still die from a mortal injury. Some injuries are so severe that the nano machines aren't capable of repairing the damage before you die."

Alexis let out a giant yawn.

Ryuu stood, "We will let you rest. Your body still needs time to recover from its ordeal."

He walked towards the door and Ladon stood to follow. Alexis reached out and snagged his hand.

"Could you stay? I don't want to be alone."

She sounded like a frightened child, but she wouldn't tell Ladon that she was terrified the nightmares would come back. Ladon studied her face for a moment, then nodded his head once and sat back down by her bedside. Secure in the knowledge that she wasn't alone, Alexis closed her eyes and drifted off into sleep.

A monster.... That is what had to be hiding in the dark.

She was standing on misty moors, but the further she tried to look into the distance the more absolute the darkness became. She was afraid of what was hidden in that inky blackness.

She walked, the small circle of light following her with each step. It wasn't long before people appeared in her line of vision—a great long line as far as the eye could see. She could make out the features and faces of those nearest her, but those further up the line were simply silhouettes that faded into the darkness.

She didn't know why, but those further away felt older, as if they were from some past generation. Instinctively, Alexis's mind deduced that those faded silhouettes had already passed on. All at once Alexis felt the death those of millions who seemed to parade into the dark only to be destroyed.

She pulled at the arms of a woman and man in her circle of light. Alexis knew that they were still alive, but they wouldn't be if they continued walking the line. But they would not stop their forward progress. Alexis begged and pleaded to no avail.

"Fafnir calls," the couple said. One by one the entire line took up the chant.

"Fafnir calls."

"Fafnir calls."

Until the entire multitude thundered in the mist-shrouded dark.

In the distance, a great roar was heard, and a monstrous shape undulated through the darkened air. Alexis didn't want the shape to find her. She knew that this was a dream, but her mind still cried out that if that thing found her they would be connected.

"Wake up, damn it!" she cried out to herself as the monster came closer

Alexis bolted awake with a scream. The last imaged burned into her mind was the glittering of white iridescent scales.

Ladon grabbed her face and forced her unfocused eyes to look at him.

"Are you with me?" Ladon's fiery golden eyes glittered with concern as the wild look faded from Alexis's own blue eyes.

Alexis sobbed and clung to Ladon. This scared Ladon almost as much as the coma she had been in these past weeks. Alexis wasn't the type to seek comfort from others. She was too independent for that. Whatever she experienced in her dream state had shaken her to her core.

Ladon worried that this out-of-character Alexis was the result of her integration ordeal. Perhaps he should talk to Ryuu about it. The black dragon might be annoyingly knowledgeable, but it did have its uses.

Alexis slowly calmed down as Ladon

absently stroked her hair and back. When her crying had subsided, she just stayed there wrapped in Ladon's arms. She melted against him and sighed. Ladon knew that she felt safe in his arms. It wasn't the declaration of love he longed for, but it was a start.

Alexis's breathing became even once again as her body fell back into an exhausted sleep. Ladon gently laid her back onto the bed, so as not to wake her. He tucked the blanket up around her chin and brushed a stray curl away from her face. She was so beautiful. Not just physically but her core self was beautiful. She was strong, independent...she could easily stand on her own, despite the fact that she loved people and truly cared about those she allowed into her circle. She had taken her role of teacher and mentor seriously even though it hadn't been the job she really wanted. Ladon smiled as he remembered the last-minute phone calls from students before they had left for the island. She had taken time, even though her schedule was packed full, to reassure them and arrange the help they needed from a distance. She was a treasure worth guarding.

But this was why something about her nightmares disturbed him. Her naturally strong mind made his connection to her nano machines tenuous at best, but he received brief flashes from her nightmares while he had tried to wake her. Those flashes had stirred something long forgotten. It was familiar, and he knew that it had something to do with the time right before they had fallen into stasis. But he still couldn't remember what it was he had forgotten, and it was beginning to frustrate him. He had a feeling that what he couldn't remember is extremely important.

*****

"I'm telling you, Ryuu, that whatever happened right before we went into stasis is the key to all of this." Ladon paced back and forth in front of the seated Ryuu. "What's more…I think that somehow Alexis tapped into something that is lost in my memory and it gave her nightmares."

"It is possible that the nano machines that you transferred to her carried some information from your memories; but what makes you think that? You said yourself while she was unconscious that you couldn't get a read from her nano machines, and when you first met she was able to shut down your nanos to prevent you from reading her brainwaves."

"All of that is true, but for just a second or two I caught a glimpse of her nightmare a little while ago. It seemed strangely familiar and…dangerous, for a lack of a better word."

"It may have been a reflexive action of one mate calling to another in times of distress. The dangerous feeling could just have been Alexis's own emotional state." Ryuu sipped on his coffee. This mated business made dragons crazy evidently. It was a good thing he didn't have a mate at the moment. Somebody had to stay on task.

"But why did it feel so familiar?"

Ryuu shrugged at Ladon. He didn't have all the answers after all.

Ladon plopped down into a chair only to pop up almost immediately and rush to the door. Ryuu turned to see a pale Alexis leaning against the door frame breathing heavily. Her body hadn't yet recovered from the coma she woke up from barely twenty-four hours before.

Ladon scooped her up and glared at Ryuu until he vacated the most comfortable chair in the room. Carefully Ladon placed Alexis in the chair and pulled another to sit next to her.

"I've had a thought," Alexis said once everyone was seated again. "We've been trying to figure out what happened long ago through the lens of the Drakonians, or dragons. But we can assume that any Drakonians on Earth at the time all of this happened fell into stasis like you did."

"That is a reasonable assumption," Ryuu conceded.

"I think I know where you are going with this," Ladon said. "If no Drakonians were left there wouldn't be a direct record of what happened." He thought for a bit. "But doesn't that leave us without a way to figure out what happened?"

"Directly, perhaps," Alexis said with a nod. "But you are thinking only in terms of Drakonians. There was another species here at that time as well…humans."

"But we only found a few years of census information after we fell into stasis before it appears that is stopped altogether." Ryuu hated to punch holes in her theory, but he had searched the entire library as she lay in a coma. He found that the library seemed to have been abandoned less than ten years after they had fallen into stasis.

"Here at the library…yes, we have precious little information. But you are thinking too literally and discounting an entire history outside of this compound."

"Alexis, I hate to agree with Ryuu, but

humanity doesn't even acknowledge that dragons ever existed. We searched your historical records before coming back to this library for information."

"That's your problem…you studied history, not mythology." Alexis smiled at the men's dumbfounded looks.

"Those are just stories…" Ryuu growled in frustration.

"But even myths have a gain of truth in them." She turned to Ryuu, "Didn't you tell me that your nano machines preferred working with water the same way Ladon's prefer fire?"

"Yes."

"Ryuu in Japanese mythology was the god of the sea, who also happened to be a dragon." She turned to Ladon. "Ladon was a dragon in Greek mythology that guarded the golden apples, though I am not sure how that relates to you."

Ryuu barked a laugh and Ladon looked down and actually blushed. Alexis looked back and forth between the two men.

"Okay, what am I missing," she said with crossed arms.

Ryuu wiped a tear of amusement from his eye and said, "Ladon was infamous for giving out a solid gold apple as a gift to the handmaidens who were particularly enthusiastic in the bedroom. It was a rather coveted prize and one only he and his genetic line could give."

"Why is that?"

"Most Drakonian nano machines are only able to manipulate one planetary element, if any at all. You need to understand that I am using element in a more ancient sense, not the periodic table kind of sense," Ryuu explained.

"So you are referring to earth, water, wind, fire, and heart or soul, right?" Alexis filed away this information for use later.

"Exactly. As I said, most only have an affinity for one, but some bloodlines contain certain nano machines that have an affinity for more than one. No one is quite sure why. It might be some sort of genetic quirk that allows the machines to reach more of their potential." Ryuu had fallen fully into lecture mode. Ladon groaned, but Alexis seemed riveted. "I don't know if it is still the case or not, but back in our day, Drakonian society had a definitive hierarchy, and it was based on the abilities of the nano machines. This led to certain bloodlines being considered nobles and even royalty. The ruling bloodline was always able to control three or more elements. The nobles two. Those that served noble houses, one. The commoners could only use their nanos to control aspects of themselves, such as healing and aging."

"So why does that make Ladon the only one who could give the golden apples?" Alexis asked.

Ladon sighed, "He's telling you in a roundabout way that I was considered a noble of Drakos because I could control fire and the earth spoke to me, which made it a simple matter for me to find veins of gold and jewels easily and forge them into something I could give as a gift."

"So the part of the myth where the Hesperides found your still-twitching body was probably from when you fell into stasis. So, who were the Hesperides? Since I doubt they were truly nymphs of the evening."

"They were three sisters who happened to be among Ladon's favorite handmaidens. They were known to be quite wild and experimentive." Ryuu chuckled. "Despite the fact that they were willing to entertain any Drakos that visited, they still managed to hoard a vast number of golden apples. They also had a cousin…she wasn't technically a handmaid, but she would visit. What was her name Ladon?"

"Arethusa. Man, I remember she was a limber thing. She could do this thing where she would throw her leg up over…" Ladon trailed off as he realized that Alexis was glaring at him. "What?" he asked, genuinely confused. She couldn't be jealous, the women he was talking about had been dead for thousands of years, but Alexis was upset about something.

Alexis stared at Ladon in silence. He wished during this time that Alexis's mind wasn't as strong as it was so he could connect to her nanos and figure out what she was thinking. After was seemed like an eternity, the spell was broken and Alexis turned to look at Ryuu. Ladon knew he shouldn't be jealous, but he couldn't help the punch in his gut when she looked away like she was dismissing him.

"I feel that we have drifted off topic a bit," Alexis stated primly. "The point that I was trying to make is that human myth contains grains of truth in it. I found Ladon on a dig in Wales. That area has a myth of a battle between a red dragon and a white dragon…Fire and ice." Alexis noticed both men frowned when she mentioned a white dragon. "In that myth the white dragon tried to enslave and destroy the people until the red dragon, who felt the people were under his protection, challenged the white dragon. It is the myth of *Y Ddraig Goch.* It is such an important myth to that region that even today the red dragon is used as the nation's symbol."

Alexis paused, hoping that the two dragons sitting with her would offer insights on the foundations of this myth like they had the others, but both remained stubbornly silent.

"In the myth, the red dragon battled and defeated the white dragon, locking him away in the ground before falling into an eternal sleep himself in his lair." Alexis knew in her heart that this myth was the key. It didn't feel like coincidence that the other dragon myths had a basis in real events. Besides, a white dragon kept coming up…in the myth, in her nightmare.

"Who is Fafnir?" Alexis demanded.

"Where did you learn of that name?" The normally calm Ryuu growled at her. "That name should have been erased from the annals of history."

Alexis was tired of being kept in the dark. These two claimed that the alien cooties that Ladon gave her somehow made her Drakonian just like them. So they didn't have a right to keep their history, even the unpleasant parts, from her.

She was just about to launch into a lecture about that very thing when a disorienting sensation over took her. Alexis's head spun to the point that she almost fell out of her chair. As it was she had to concentrate to keep what little food she had in her stomach down. She closed her eyes until the world quit its whirlwind. When she opened her eyes again, she found her vision split; one side was observing the world around her like normal while the other had numerous images flashing through it at speeds so fast that she could barely hold on to any of them. Yet even in those flashing images she had the impression of several brutal images involving a white dragon and a pale man she didn't recognize. She strained to slow down the images to see more.

"Enough!"

Ryuu's cry of pain broke Alexis concentration, and suddenly the images stopped as the world spun around her once more. This time when she opened her eyes, only the present world appeared. Both men were holding their heads in their hands.

"By the stars, she is powerful," Ryuu groaned.

"I couldn't shut down her nanos and they smashed through every barrier my own erected,"

Ladon sighed as he rubbed his temples.

"Same here. I've never heard of a transformed mate being able to do such things." Ryuu closed his eyes and leaned back in his chair.

"What the hell was that?" Alexis demanded.

"It would seem, my dear, that you are able to control the element of the heart and soul. While all Drakos can use their nanos to glean information from the minds of species who do not have nanos, only a select few can enter the minds of other Drakos. Normally the nano machines would be at a stalemate unless invited in." Ryuu sighed and rubbed his temple. "You, however, managed to not only shut our nano defenses down, you seemed to have left a doorway that you can use to contact us at any time. With training, you probably could even control the actions of the individual whose mind you invade. Ladon said you naturally had a strong mind, as you shut his nanos down the first day you met, but I think even he underestimated you."

"I don't want to control anyone." Alexis's eyes glistened. Too many changes too fast. "I just don't want to be left in the dark."

"Then I guess we need to tell you about Fafnir." Ladon got up from his chair and walked towards the kitchen. "You should eat first because you may not want to after you hear the tale of Fafnir."

After a filling meal of a simple stew and bread, the men spent the next few hours talking about a dragon named Fafnir. They had been right about the story causing the loss of appetite. This Fafnir had been the Dr. Mengele of the Drakonian race. The fact that he was considered minor royalty because of his ability to control fire, water, and the mind via his nano machines kept him from the harshest penalties for a while.

Ladon told her how the man had been banished from the Drakos home world instead of imprisoned or executed. It was obvious that Ladon hated the man. Even the even-keeled Ryuu bristled at the mention of his atrocities.

Fafnir made his way to earth and found a large population that considered the Drakos to be divine beings. He used this to his advantage to continue his experiments. The bloody rituals of human sacrifice in ancient cultures around the planet had their roots in Fafnir's experiments. Alexis could see the roots of the Norse myth in the descriptions of Fafnir's character. He was a psychopath with a selfish streak a mile wide. He didn't even try to hide his ugliness. He was just like the Norse myth in that regard...a deadly monster that viewed everything in his sight as rightfully his.

"Thank the gods that monster is dead by now," Ladon spat.

"Why are you so certain he is dead?" Alexis asked.

"Drakonians are long lived, but we are not immortal. Even we reach a point where we cannot renew our nano machines as efficiently and we age...eventually to pass on, which is the proper way of the universe," Ryuu explained. "No dragon in history has lived longer than two thousand years. The only reason that Ladon and I are alive is because our bodies were in stasis during that time."

"Maybe Fafnir was in stasis too," Alexis pointed out.

Ladon shook his head. "The battle in the Welsh myth happened. Fafnir had wiped out entire fledgling civilizations on this planet, and he had moved into what you now call Europe. The various other Drakonians stationed here were simple soldiers and scholars; they couldn't touch a royal, even the black sheep of that bloodline. I was a noble, so I held more clout and was informed by the royal family that I was to confine Fafnir and they would collect him. They had finally decided that he had to be controlled instead of just banished."

"But didn't being a royal make him more powerful? Wasn't he able to perform mind control?" Alexis remembered the flashes of a fierce battle in her mind.

Ladon winced. "Alexis, until we can help you to control your nanos, could you please refrain from trying to dig for answers before we have a chance to explain them to you."

"Sorry. I thought I was remembering something from earlier."

"You were, but when you did it activated your nanos to try and find more information…not just the ones in your body, but the ones you left in mine as well."

"Fascinating…." Alexis gazed on Ladon with an academic's eyes. For a moment, he saw the fiery passion for knowledge above all else that he had also seen in the monster they were talking about. But where the monster would have continued to inflict discomfort just to see how far he could take it, Alexis, though curious, concentrated, and he felt her nanos go dormant just as he requested.

"As I was saying…I was tasked with containing Fafnir until the royal guard could arrive to collect him. It was a fierce battle. We both were adept with fire. I preferred the heat, him the absence of it. He liked the irony of burning with cold. He would couple the lack of heat with his mastery of water and create ice to use as missiles. I still have a few scars from those."

Ladon stopped to collect himself. It took everything in Alexis not to try and prompt him to continue. She could see that the memories were still difficult for him. She briefly wondered if dragons suffered from PTSD.

"The answer to your question is that yes,

Fafnir has a knack for mind control. He used the humans as cannon fodder in our battle. Men, women…even children…it didn't matter to him. A few of the Drakonians even became his unwilling guard. I had to maim and destroy those I considered friends and family to end his reign of terror."

Alexis's logical mind quickly went to the most efficient conclusion. "Why didn't he just control you instead?"

Ladon grinned but it didn't reach his eyes. "I may not have the talent for controlling others, but I made a point of strengthening my own nanos against any invasions of the mind. It wouldn't do for the general of armies to fall victim to an enemy's control. So while it took a lot of energy, I was able to withstand Fafnir's attacks, much to his frustration."

"Which is why your ability to smash through those cultivated barriers so easily is such a surprise to us. The sheer raw power of your nanos, especially with how new they are, is amazing," Ryuu interjected. "When you learn control, you will be a truly formidable woman."

"I still don't see how all of this would explain why Fafnir has to be dead," Alexis questioned.

Ladon shrugged. "I don't have clear memories of what happened right before we fell into stasis, but I clearly remember Fafnir being picked up by the royal guard. He wasn't on the planet when those of us here ended up in stasis.

Bloodlines are connected by our nano machines. Even when on different planets we feel a certain connection to each other. I do not feel any of my former family, so I must assume they are dead. If those that were off planet from that time are dead, I can only assume that Fafnir also numbers among them. He wasn't the youngest of dragons even then."

"You can't tell for certain?" Alexis asked.

"He's not of my bloodline, so no."

Alexis frowned. She knew it wasn't reasonable, but she was fairly certain that Fafnir was still alive. Her nightmares felt too real. She knew without a doubt that the deaths she had felt were real and some were recent. But she also knew without proof she wouldn't be able to convince Ryuu and Ladon. Hell, she wouldn't have believed it either based simple on a recurring nightmare if she hadn't felt it herself.

Alexis turned to Ryuu. "Has anything else

useful been located while I was ill?"

She needed to get back to civilization so she could research the Fafnir myths to see if she could possibly learn something more. While her mind made a list of things she needed to start her research, a yawn crawled out of her mouth. The trio had been talking for a few hours now, and he body was screaming for more rest. She would be glad when her stamina returned.

Ladon noticed the yawn. "Alexis needs to eat something and then get some more sleep."

Alexis started to protest that she was fine when Ladon cut her off with a gentle kiss. "Let me take care of you, Alexis."

How could one argue with that kind of request? So she just nodded and allowed herself to be led off in search of food.

Ladon found Ryuu going over the census papers after he had tucked Alexis back into bed.

"I wonder why Alexis was so interested in that butcher," Ladon asked as he sat and pulled a stack of scrolls towards him. He wasn't as fluent in as many ancient Earth languages as Ryuu was, but he could read some.

Ryuu shrugged. "It's human nature to examine the brutality of life."

"But she knew his name."

"Maybe she came across it in one of the

manuscripts."

Ladon was about to argue that impossibility—after all, they had destroyed every record of Fafnir's existence—when Alexis's scream echoed down the corridor.

Both men knocked over their chairs in a scramble to get to her. The bolted down the corridor until they made it to Alexis's bedroom.

Ladon pushed Ryuu out of the way and ran to the bed. Alexis was thrashing and screaming. Another nightmare. Ladon looked helplessly to Ryuu as he sat on the bed to gather up the woman he loved. He somehow felt like her nightmares were his fault. They had started after he completed the mating ritual. Ladon was truly worried that something had gone wrong and the nanos or the fever somehow damaged her mind.

Once he had Alexis in his arms, she started to fight him in her sleep.

"I won't go…I won't go…."

Ladon had to grab the fist that flew at his face to prevent Alexis from breaking his nose. He retained a grip on both hands as she struggled.

"Alexis, wake up!"

Alexis seemed to be stuck in her dream world. Despite Ladon shaking her and yelling, still her eyes remained closed and she struggled.

"Ryuu, help me…she isn't waking up," Ladon frantically called.

Ryuu sat behind Alexis while Ladon kept a firm grip on her thrashing. He knew that Ladon was worried that Alexis's mind was damaged from the conversion, but Ryuu was beginning to wonder if something else might be going on. He had a suspicion that a truly damaged mind wouldn't form coherent nightmares, nor would it be able to maintain logical thought during her waking hours. Of course, this was only conjecture since it had been only a short time since she woke from her coma. He decided to test his hypothesis and instead of shaking her awake he calmly talked into her ear.

"Build a wall, Alexis. Brick by brick. With each row, the images will be pushed from your mind. Lock them away. Your mind is yours alone. No one has permission to enter unless you allow it. You threw Ladon from your mind when you first met. You are even stronger now. No one can withstand your will. Build the wall. Close them out."

With each quiet set of directions, Alexis calmed more and more. The screaming stopped.

The thrashing ceased. Her breathing became calm and even until finally her eyes fluttered open and locked onto Ladon's.

Tears glittered in her eyes, which caused Ladon to crush her to him in a tight hold. She held on to his shirt like she was afraid he would disappear.

"Fafnir's alive, Ladon…I don't know how I know. I just do," Alexis choked out between sobs. "He knows I am here. He is coming for me. He can't find you too. You have to leave me."

"Hush," Ladon squeezed her tighter. "I would never leave you, Alexis. You are mine."

Alexis pulled away and looked into Ladon's eyes. "You don't understand…."

"I don't have to understand to know that my place is here by your side. Let me get you some chamomile tea. You need to rest so you can get your strength back."

Ladon caressed her cheek and stood. Alexis didn't miss the worried look he tossed Ryuu's way as he headed for the kitchen. Ladon thought she was losing her mind.

Alexis looked over to Ryuu to see him

studying her.

"I'm not crazy, Ryuu."

"I didn't say you were."

"Ladon thinks I am."

"He's just worried, Alexis. We both are."

Alexis shook her head, "You have to get him to believe me, Ryuu. He has to be prepared for what is coming."

Ryuu looked thoughtful. "Tell me about your nightmares. That is where you learned about Fafnir isn't it?"

Alexis nodded and sighed. "When I was in the coma, I could hear you and Ladon. Especially when you were talking to me. But I was lost in the darkness. At first I wandered alone. Then I felt excruciating pain—pain so bad that it stole my voice from me. I couldn't even scream. Then the pain subsided and I felt the presence of others…faint at first but then they got stronger. With each wave of pain, I felt more people and they became more distinct. At first it was comforting; I wasn't alone anymore. Then I realized that many of those I felt were from the past. I don't know how to explain it, but I felt their deaths, and they were hard deaths.

Thousands...maybe even millions of deaths and I felt every one. That was when the dream became a nightmare. Do you have any idea what it is like to experience dying on that scale? I'm not talking about just knowing they were dead in some abstract number...I'm talking about feeling their pain, terror, their last breath. I experienced it all."

"That doesn't tell me about Fafnir," Ryuu prompted. He had to get Alexis to finish the tale before Ladon returned or the fire dragon would beat him to death just for the pale look of terror in Alexis's eyes.

"The souls, for lack of a better word, were marching in a line into the darkness and I instinctively knew a monster lived there. I tried to stop a few of the ones that still felt 'alive' to me. That is when I heard the name Fafnir."

"What happened tonight?"

"A white dragon appeared in my circle of light. It said, 'I found you.'" Alexis shivered. "It felt evil."

Ladon came through the door before Ryuu could ask Alexis to clarify her statement. Ladon had her drink the tea and tucked her back into bed. Ryuu watched as a metaphorical wall came up between the pair. Ladon's worry for Alexis's sanity was hurting her and he didn't even realize it.

The men left Alexis to get more sleep. As they walked down the hall, Ryuu put a hand on Ladon's arm, stopping his forward movement.

"I don't think Alexis is crazy, Ladon."

Ladon shook off Ryuu's arm. "You don't seriously think that Fafnir is still alive, do you? It's impossible."

"I don't know." Ryuu tugged at his dark hair in frustration. "But I don't think her mind is damaged."

"Then why is she having these crazy nightmares?" Ladon threw his hands in the air. "That is not normal."

The pair continued their way down the hall. They both needed to get some sleep themselves soon or they wouldn't be able to function either.

Ryuu looked sideways at Ladon. "You know the fact that you don't believe what she is saying is hurting Alexis."

"Don't you think I know that, Ryuu?" Ladon growled. "But if I give in to her delusions I'm afraid she will get worse."

"What if they aren't delusions?"

Ladon stopped so suddenly that Ryuu nearly walked into his back. The fire dragon whipped around on his friend in anger.

"Don't you think I would love to have a logical explanation for her nightmares? Or this fixation on Fafnir? Do you really think that I want the woman I love more than life itself to be going crazy?"

Ryuu studied his friend and decided that maybe it was time for some tough love. "Do you actually want to know what I think?" he challenged.

Ladon's voice raised, "Yeah I do."

"Fine. I think you are afraid. You forget I saw you after your battle with Fafnir. You almost didn't survive. I think it is safer for you to think that he is dead and your mate is insane than it is to think you might have to face the man who nearly ended your life again." Ryuu poked Ladon's chest to punctuate each accusation.

Ladon roared and took a swing at the black dragon's face. Ryuu knew Ladon's temper was near the surface and was prepared for the punch. He ducked and sent his leg out to sweep Ladon off balance.

The pair had sparred many times and were familiar with each other's fighting style. But Ladon wasn't sparring. His anger and guilt had finally hit a boiling point; he needed to smash something, and Ryuu made the perfect target.

They wrestled and crashed the rest of the way down the hall. It was a small miracle that Alexis didn't come out to investigate the commotion. Though she was an intelligent woman and probably knew better than to get between two battling dragons.

Ladon landed a lucky shot and knocked Ryuu's head back, causing him to fall into the giant open space of the flight deck. This pissed off the black dragon and he transformed to his hulking dragon form, shredding his clothes in the process. He swiped his massive spiked tail at Ladon, who launched himself into the air. He transformed midleap and landed fully transformed nearby.

The thunderous roar of battling dragons shook the island mountain compound. Ryuu knew that the only thing saving him from serious harm was the fact that he and Ladon were friends. That didn't mean that the fire dragon wouldn't make him feel it though. Ryuu made sure to get in a fair number of blows himself.

Soon the ridiculousness of the entire situation struck Ryuu as being funny, and he fumbled a few swipes of his claws as his dragon shook with mirth. That opened an opportunity for Ladon to pin the black dragon, who quickly transformed into a laughing man.

Ladon transformed still on top of Ryuu. "Are you laughing? Why are you laughing?"

Ryuu shoved at the still naked Ladon on top of him, "Get off of me, you perv."

Ladon rolled off of is friend and flopped on the ground beside him. "Why are we fighting?"

"Because you are an ass."

"Alexis says I'm always an ass."

"Well, she's not wrong."

Ladon reached over and punched Ryuu in the shoulder without even looking over.

"Ow. I've got bruises all over my body thanks to you."

"They'll be gone by morning, you big baby."

"I'm a scholar, not a fighter."

Ladon sighed. "Yeah you are. You've forgotten more than I will ever know." He turned his head and looked at Ryuu. "You really think that Alexis's nightmare are something other than damage to her mind, don't you?"

Ryuu's black eyes stared steadily into Ladon's golden ones. "I do."

Ladon turned his eyes back to the ceiling. "Shit, I thought you might say that."

"You know there might be a way to prove it definitively."

"Come on, people! We need to get a move on. The plane will be at the airstrip within the hour."

Ladon was in full general mode and Alexis was about ready to kill him. The men had burst into her room in the middle of the night to demand that she start packing. Alexis's body still felt exhausted because the nightmares hadn't let her get the restorative rest she needed.

Ryuu was in his dragon form as Ladon strapped a few more items to his back before he launched himself into the air. Alexis laid her head against the last stack of equipment. Ryuu would be returning shortly to watch over her as Ladon flew this stack of things down the mountain in his dragon form. Neither of the men had told why there was such a sense of urgency.

She was wondering if Ladon was going to force her into some form of mental therapy because of the nightmares. Alexis turn her head to watch the clouds pass in shades of pink and purple. The opening of the dragon landing pad was so vast that it almost felt like she was floating among the clouds. She sighed because peaceful moments like these were going to be few and far between—because she knew her nightmares were real.

Maybe it would be best to be locked away from the two men she had come to care a great deal about. If Fafnir didn't know about them, they would be safe. She had built the mental wall again, but it weakened each time she fell asleep, so she would have to reconstruct it when she woke up. She never knew that a mental battle could be so physically exhausting. She wanted to close her eyes and try to get some sleep, but she forced her body to stay awake until the men deposited her wherever they were going to leave her. She didn't even care at this point where it was as long as it was away from

Ladon and Ryuu—especially Ladon.

Alexis felt great puffs of wind long before she saw the shimmering black wings of Ryuu. Ryuu landed and changed with graceful practice. Alexis knew that she should blush at the sight of someone she considered a close friend walking her direction completely nude. Both dragons seemed very comfortable in their nudity, a byproduct of their transformation, she supposed. Alexis wasn't sexually attracted to Ryuu, but that didn't mean she couldn't appreciate a fine form when she saw one.

Alexis watched Ladon strip in preparation for his transformation. Now her reaction to his nudity was a hell of a lot more than just appreciation of form. Her body suddenly felt feverish, and she couldn't help but remember the feel of his hands and mouth on her body.

When Ladon turned to give her a wolfish grin with a waggle of eyebrow, she knew that she had been projecting through her nano machines. So she concentrated on sending him an image of her kicking him in the shins. The corner of her lips lifted a bit at Ladon's bark of laughter.

She watched as Ladon transformed. He was a magnificent dragon. His deep red scales glinted almost like facetted jewels. But despite the reptilian slit to the pupil, the eyes always remained Ladon's, with that fiery golden color that Alexis had only ever experienced in his eyes.

Alexis moved away from the final stack of supplies and equipment so Ryuu could quickly secure the cargo to Ladon's massive body. Once Ladon had launched himself into the air, Ryuu walked purposefully towards Alexis.

As he neared, he reached his arms out to grab her. Alexis held up a hand to stop him and wagged her finger between the two of them.

"Uh no…this ain't happening until you put on some pants."

Ryuu chuckled. "I'm just going to pick you up so I can carry you down in dragon form. We don't have time, nor do you have the stamina, to climb down the mountain."

"I get that, Ryuu. I'm not stupid," Alexis snapped at him. "But I don't feel comfortable having my buddy hold me in his naked arms. Can't you just change and I can climb on your back or something?"

"Sure." Ryuu's mischievous grin made Alexis a bit wary, but Alexis felt that being in Ryuu's naked arms would be disrespectful to Ladon.

Besides, Ryuu was like a brother, and being held against his naked body just felt pervy.

Ryuu reverted to his dragon form. It still amazed Alexis that the men, despite being big burly guys, could change into such a massive creature. She hadn't really gotten the chance to examine them up close in dragon form. , so Alexis took a minute to look at Ryuu. His wings were covered in a thick leathery membrane. It wasn't the translucent membrane that Hollywood portrayed. No light would pass through his midnight wing. The scales were hard plates that fit snuggly together, creating a smooth texture like a snake's skin on a much larger scale.

Ryuu extended his foreleg for Alexis to use to climb up. She found that it was a little more difficult than she had first thought. It was difficult to find traction on the smooth surface of his scales. Ryuu had to lift his leg to slide Alexis onto his back. Alexis straddled Ryuu at the base of his neck.

She shimmied down until her backside was seated between his shoulders and her legs dangled in front of his wing joint. Alexis could have sworn that Ryuu shivered and purred as she moved around, trying to find a comfortable spot.

Alexis leaned forward and held on to Ryuu's

massive neck as best she could.

"Okay. I'm ready."

Ryuu took her at her word and lumbered over to the opening. Instead of the running launch that he and Ladon seemed to prefer, Ryuu simply leaned over the edge until they were falling through the air.

Alexis squeezed her arms and legs against Ryuu to prevent herself from being unseated. Again, she swore she felt the massive beast rumble a purr deep in his chest. Just as Alexis was about to scream in terror as the ocean waves filled her vision, Ryuu spread his midnight wings and caught an updraft.

It took a minute for Alexis's stomach to return to her, but when it did she looked around her in awe. The library's island looked like a hidden paradise from the air. With the exception of the original climb to get to the library, Alexis hadn't seen any of the island outside of the library complex. The complex was hidden in the single mountain peak that dominated the island. Except for the highest peaks, a verdant forest surrounded the mountain. One side of the island was a little flatter, with meadows interspersed with the trees. It was here that the airstrip was located. The entire island was surrounded by the bluest water Alexis had ever seen. It was so clear that she could see a pod of whales clearly beneath the surface swimming by the island.

Ryuu banked to the right, swinging them around to the other side of the island. His descent was leisurely, giving Alexis time to enjoy the natural beauty around them. She could see why Ryuu had settled in such a place. She imagined what it must have looked like with a multitude of dragons filling the sky.

All too soon, their flight was over, as Ryuu gently landed next to the air strip. Alexis slid from Ryuu's back with a grin.

"That was awesome!" Alexis jumped up and down in excitement when she saw Ladon stalking towards them. "Ladon!"

Alexis ran to him, wanting to share her excitement with him only to have him put her aside with a frown.

Ladon stomped over to Ryuu as the dragon returned to a man. As soon as the transformation was complete, Ladon punched Ryuu in the face.

"She is mine!" Ladon shouted at the black dragon. "What were you thinking carrying her on your back?"

"Whoa! Wait a minute. I asked him to carry

me on his back. Even if I hadn't, you don't own me, Ladon." Alexis grabbed Ladon's arm to pull him away from Ryuu. She wasn't prepared for the stark look of hurt and betrayal in his eyes. She took a step back as if she had been hit with a physical blow.

Ladon threw Ryuu's clothes at him and turned and walked away. Every muscle in his body was tight with caged rage.

Alexis started to go after him when a hand on her shoulder stopped her.

"Let him be for a bit, Alexis. He needs to calm down." Ryuu had put his pants and boots on and was in the process of putting his shirt on.

"I don't understand what just happened."

Ryuu sighed, "A bad joke that backfired." Ryuu sat on the ground and patted a soft tuft of grass next to him. "I used your ignorance of Drakonian culture to try to get under Ladon's skin a bit. I'm sorry."

Alexis sat down and frowned at Ryuu. "From the looks of things I would say that you definitely got under Ladon's skin. The question is why?"

"Well…." Ryuu scratched his chin and stalled until Alexis's glare convinced him to continue. "When we are in dragon form normally only mates would be allowed to ride on our backs...at the very least someone we were involved with sexually."

"Oh my god! Does Ladon think we have had sex?"

Ryuu shook his head with a slight grin, "Despite his temper, Ladon is actually very intelligent. He knows that you and I haven't had sex. He was pissed at me for a different reason."

Alexis crossed her arms and raised an eyebrow at him expectantly.

Ryuu groaned and mumbled something that Alexis wasn't sure she heard correctly.

"What was that?" she questioned.

"I said that a woman on a dragon's back can be sexually arousing."

Alexis punched him in the arm. "So that purring I felt was you getting off?" Alexis scrunched up her face, "I didn't want you to carry me in your arms because you were naked and that would just be weird. And now...eww...now I feel like I have a pervy little brother."

Ryuu stood up and offered a hand to Alexis. "So you think of me like a brother, huh?"

Alexis took his hand and let him pull her on to her feet. "Yeah, so?"

Ryuu grinned, "That means you love me." He drew out the word love like an annoying brother would do.

"No, it means I find you annoying. All brothers are annoying; it is in the sibling handbook somewhere," Alexis huffed. "You are the bane of my existence."

The pair started walking towards the piles of supplies and equipment as they teased back and forth.

"You love me."

"Annoying."

Ryuu bumped Alexis's shoulder, "I'm the big brother. I can't be annoying." His voice raised to grandiose proportions, "I shall guide and protect my little sister from the world."

"Annnd annoying."

Alexis turned and walked away from Ryuu.

She needed to find Ladon and let him know that she now understood why he was upset. She needed him to know that she hadn't meant to hurt him.

Ryuu cheerfully called after Alexis, "You know I think I might be developing a sister complex."

"I think I might let Ladon eat you after all," she smiled back.

She left with Ryuu's laugh echoing in her ears.

The flight off the island was a silent affair.
Ladon knew that he shouldn't be angry with Alexis.
She hadn't known Drakonian customs. Despite this
mess being Ryuu's fault, he couldn't really work up
a good mad at him either. Honestly, if the roles had
been reversed Ladon had to admit that he probably
would have pulled a similar stunt.

Despite all of the logical self-discussion,
Ladon was still upset. A single phrase carelessly
thrown out by Alexis had knocked him completely
off kilter: 'You don't own me.' Didn't she

understand that she was his? Alexis may not realize it, but she already owned every part of Ladon. Now Ladon was terrified that Alexis may not reciprocate his feelings. Just because he completed the ritual and gave her body the nano machines that converted her into a true Drakonian bride, that didn't mean that she had to love him. True she had to feel something or the nanos wouldn't have successfully integrated, but that still didn't guarantee that she would love him. And even if she did love him in the beginning, once the nanos were fully active she could come to hate him and it would change nothing because those machines were now hers not his.

Ladon closed his eyes and rubbed the bridge of his nose. He was talking himself in circles and, in the end, it didn't matter. Alexis had apologized for the dragon ride. If he couldn't let go of it, the wall between them would just get higher.

He looked out the window of the private jet. The landscape had changed from blues and greens to great white expanses. They had to be careful to fly under the radar because this was not an authorized flight into a foreign country. They hadn't had time to get through the red tape within the Russian government before heading to the tundra. Ryuu had also pointed out that if this facility was still buried within the glaciers of Siberia that it would be best if the human governments didn't know of its existence.

To that end, they planned on touching down in a tiny village that housed only a few dozen people. From there they would take dog sleds to get to the coordinates.

Ladon let his eyes wander to Alexis. The circles beneath her eyes were even more bruised, her skin a sickly shade of pale. He knew that she wasn't getting proper rest, but looking at her now Ladon knew that if something didn't change soon her body would just collapse, even with the aid of her nanos.

Ladon knew why they couldn't take Alexis to a human hospital, and he hoped that Tugarin's research facility was still intact. He wasn't sold on the idea that Fafnir was somehow attacking her mind, but maybe they could fix the malfunctioning nanos and save Alexis's sanity. Once she was safe and well then he could court her like she deserved.

Alexis finally nodded off. She had asked Ladon to wake her if she fell asleep, but she was so exhausted that Ladon just couldn't bring himself to do so. He watched her as she slept. Physically she was so delicate—tiny in stature and almost fragile looking. Her curves gave her a soft appearance. The deep contrast between her pale skin and nearly black hair made her striking. When her deep blue eyes sparkled at you, she became mesmerizing. And the beauty of it all was she had no idea of the real impact she had on the males of the species.

Ladon reached over to brush a wild curl from her face. Just as his fingers brushed across her skin, Alexis's eyes snapped open and she grabs his wrist in an iron grip.

Ladon has never seen Alexis's eyes look so malevolent. Her lips curl into a vicious parody of a smile as she twisted Ladon's arm away from her. Ladon struggled in vain to twist his arm out of Alexis's bruising grip, but she just squeezed harder. Ladon grimaced as he felt the bones of his wrist starting to crack.

"Alexis, you need to let me go," Ladon said through clenched teeth.

Alexis gave a huffing laugh. "So you managed to survive, you impudent noble."

The voice that emerged from Alexis's mouth wasn't her own. It was deeper, more masculine, and held a note that seemed so familiar to Ladon.

"Who are you?" Ladon's voice rose with the demand.

"Bow before your master."

Alexis squeezed his wrist harder, and Ladon had to concentrate not to cry out in pain as his bones broke. Don't show the enemy weakness; that was a lesson he had learned early in life.

"I have no master," growled Ladon. The commotion had Ryuu coming out of the cockpit, where he had been talking with the pilot.

"Such a proud fire dragon. The only one who ever truly stood against me, except for the female here." A malevolent laugh erupted from Alexis's delicate mouth. "She tried to elude me. Even when I finally found her, she kept her knowledge of your existence from me." Alexis's mouth twisted into a feral fashion. "She planned on getting locked away in a mental institution, so she would be far away from you when I came for her."

"Leave Alexis alone, you bastard!" Ladon's pupils turned to slits as his dragon fought to emerge and face the threat.

"This one will make the most interesting test subject. Already she is so strong even after being newly formed...."

"Alexis...." Ryuu's calm voice broke through the dialogue. "I know you are still in there somewhere. Remember what we told you of Fafnir?

Ladon was strong enough to keep him out of his mind. You have already proved that you are mentally stronger than Ladon. So, by extension, you are stronger than Fafnir. Push the bastard out!"

Alexis released her grip on Ladon and clutched her head in her hands. Her voice flipped back and forth between the feminine tones Ladon knew so well and the gravelly growl of the thing invading her mind.

Suddenly Alexis slumped in her seat. Ladon gingerly reached for her and sat her up. Using his good hand, he lightly patted her cheek.

"Alexis, love, are you with us?"

Her eyes fluttered open, and though exhausted, the blue eyes that gazed back at Ladon were clear and familiar.

"Do you believe me yet?" she asked, tears shimmering in her eyes.

Ladon rested his head against her forehead and breathed her in.

"Yeah, I do, love. I do."

Ryuu had worked his magic from the plane somehow, and the villagers, on the promise of massive amounts of cash, had the sled and supplies ready to go and waiting as soon at their plane touched down. Their pilot had instructions to leave Russian air space via the north pole and wait at the company-owned airstrip in Alaska. If questioned, this stop was to simply refuel, and his employers were still on the island in the south seas.

Alexis was checking the rigging on the sleds

and familiarizing herself with the dog teams. The locals had shaken their heads when the trio had refused a guide for their trek. The local elder demanded the cost of replacing the dog team and equipment in addition to the monies already paid. Ryuu wanted to argue about what amounted to extortion but Ladon just threw the cash at the man.

It would take almost seventy-two hours to reach the coordinates of the Drakonian research facility, and the stars only knew how long it would take them to figure out what needed to be done to permanently block Fafnir from Alexis's mind. She had already been awake for almost a full day. That would mean a minimum of four days without sleep for Alexis since Fafnir seemed to be able to breach her mental defenses when she slept. Even with the aid of the nano machines a body could only take so long without rest, and Ladon was afraid they would be pushing Alexis's limit.

"Are you sure this is the best option, Ryuu?" Ladon asked his friend.

"At this point I think it is our only option. Tugarin was researching the connections that the nano machines created between individual bloodlines. Hopefully we will be able to use his research to sever that connection."

"You know Fafnir will be coming for us, right?" Ladon turned to the black dragon. Ryuu could see the battle general staring back at him—a commander asking a soldier if he was ready for battle.

"I don't think Fafnir will come himself, at least not at first." Alexis heard the tail end of their conversation.

Ryuu tilted his head and frowned. "What makes you say that?"

"In all my dreams and even when he took over my mind, I got the impression that he was basically tied to one place. He was forcing the people to come to him. I'm not sure he can come for us just yet. But his minions are on the way. That much I gleaned from his mind."

"That at least gives us time to prepare." Ladon rubbed his hands together in glee. "Minions I can handle."

Alexis stared at Ladon.

"What?" Ladon frowned at her.

"It just feels kind of weird to suddenly have you believe me."

Ladon sighed. "I'm sorry, Alexis. I should have believed you, especially after Ryuu tried to tell me that there was something going on. I was an idiot. In all fairness, I will probably be an idiot again at some point."

Alexis smiled and stood on her tip toes, expectantly. When Ladon just stood there, she waved him down until she could grab his face to pull him down into a kiss."

"Apology accepted."

Ladon was stunned speechless. The wall between them seemed to crumble in an instant. He rested his hand on the small of Alexis's back and guided her towards the sled. A much as he wanted to take advantage of the renewed connection, they needed to hurry.

All three were bundled up, though, if necessary their nanos would regulate their body temperature to keep them alive. That just expended more energy and Ladon felt it prudent to conserve energy until they had a better idea of what they were dealing with.

Ryuu and Ladon would take turns driving the team, resting only when absolutely necessary. If they could keep up the brutal pace, they should be able to reach the facility in a little less than three days.

Ryuu handed a bottle of pills to Alexis as she crawled into the sled.

"What is that?"

"I had the pilot pick up a prescription for Ritalin before he came to get us."

"Why?"

Ryuu shrugged. "I knew that Alexis didn't want to sleep because that was when the nightmares came. This is basically speed. It will help to keep her awake for a few days. Not a long-term solution, but it will hopefully get us to Tugarin's place."

"I wonder if Tugarin is still there," Ladon said as he crawled in beside Alexis.

Ryuu cinched the couple into the sled, "It would be helpful if he is. He knows more about the nano technology than I ever will."

Ladon called over his shoulder as Ryuu set the team in motion. "Didn't he have a mate?"

"I thought mates were removed from the planet," Alexis said.

Ladon answered, "They were supposed to be, but Tugarin refused to go, and their pairing had produced numerous offspring, including a daughter, which was kind of a miracle in itself. The government came to a compromise. Tugarin would study why his mating was so fertile with a single woman when others rarely had children despite spreading their seed far and wide."

"So what was his mate's name?" Alexis asked.

"Zoya," Ryuu offered. "It would be great if she is there as well. That woman was the best cook in the universe. She could make anything taste like heaven."

Alexis chuckled, "I guess the adage of 'the way to a man's heart is through his stomach' crosses species."

"You don't understand; what Zoya could do with food was an art form."

Ryuu encouraged the dog team to go faster. Alexis raised her face to the wind rushing by. The air here smelled clear. The vast expanse of ice and snow surrounding them made everything feel brand new—a clean slate, like the world was waiting to be formed. It felt like a new beginning. It may have been giddiness from lack of sleep, but for the first time in days, Alexis had hope.

"Onward to Zoya and her magical kitchen," Alexis laughed.

*****

The third day on the trail was dawning. They were far enough north that, despite the time denoting day, the sun would only actually rise for a few hours around noon. The aurora in the night sky still danced. Ryuu was at the helm until Ladon woke up. The men had taken turns napping.

Alexis really wished she could nap. Her body was desperately crying out for sleep. She didn't understand why the two dragons didn't seem to be connected, since as far as she could tell it wasn't just bloodlines connected now. She could feel a connection to the rest of dragon kind, both past and present, through the white dragon. The researcher in her knew that was a significant fact, but her sleep-deprived brain was having difficulty figuring out what the implications were.

Her head really hurt. She had been able to keep Fafnir out as long as she was awake. Ryuu and Ladon assured her that at some point the nanos would automatically shield her mind, but she wasn't so sure. If constant vigilance for days wasn't enough to train them to the task, then perhaps it was beyond their scope. Despite the debilitating exhaustion, there was an advantage to the foul connection. Each time Fafnir beat against the mental fortress of her mind, she caught glimpses of his own mind. The white dragon either didn't realize that was happening or didn't care because he never took steps to block her.

She felt the now familiar push of Fafnir trying to enter her mind. Part of her wanted to close her eyes and concentrate to pull as much information as she could, but she was afraid that she would fall asleep in her exhausted state, so she had to content herself with the flashes of information that came to her.

Fafnir was trying to determine where on the planet she was. He was so certain that Ladon wouldn't be far from her, yet at the same time he was angry that he couldn't follow her connection to Ladon to get to him directly.

Alexis knew through both Ladon's and Fafnir's memories that Ladon was the only person to successfully stand in Fafnir's way. That made Ladon a man to be eliminated in his eyes.

She caught a glimpse of a group of soldiers

loading a futuristic ship and sighed. She shook
Ladon to wake him up. Ladon just grumbled and
turned away from her to continue sleeping. Alexis
frowned and cocked her elbow as far as the confines
of the furs they were bundled in would allow her.
She planted her elbow in Ladon's side. He gave a
satisfying yelp.

"What the hell?" Ladon was awake now.

"I saw something this last time Fafnir tried to
enter my mind," Alexis stated.

"Fuck. Alexis, we told you to keep him out
of your mind. That means don't enter his either,"
Ladon growled at her.

Alexis just glared at him. "What do you think
I have been trying to do for the last three days?" Her
voice raised in pitch and Ladon was taken aback by
her vehemence. "In case you haven't noticed, I'm
cracking under the strain here. I don't want to be in
his head. I don't want him in mine. But it appears
that I don't have a choice until we figure out what
the hell is up with my nano machines. And might
add that I got the defective little bastards from you."
She poked Ladon's chest with her finger hard
enough to make him wince. "So instead of barking at
me, why don't you try to listen for a change."

Ladon grabbed Alexis and pulled her into a bear hug. He held on to her anger-stiffened body until her muscles relaxed.

"I'm sorry. I didn't mean to be an ass," Ladon said.

"You are always an ass." Alexis's voice was muffled by the thick material of Ladon's coat.

His lip quirked at that proclamation, though he returned to seriousness quickly. "I just don't want that bastard anywhere near you—not even mentally. It doesn't excuse my yelling at you, but I just feel so helpless and I don't know how to act when I feel like that." He heaved a big sigh, "Go ahead and tell us what you know. I'll shut up and listen."

"I saw a ship like nothing I had ever seen before. It was like something Hollywood would dream up. I can only assume that I was seeing things through Fafnir's eyes. There was a squad of soldiers being loaded into the ship. I don't know how, but I know that they are heading for Earth and are looking for me and hopefully Ladon." Alexis turned her head towards Ryuu. "He doesn't really see you as a threat, but he is afraid of Ladon. And I feel his need for vengeance."

Ladon's hand reached out and cupped

Alexis's chin. He turned her head so her eyes were looking at him.

"How many soldiers did you see, Alexis? Can you tell if they are Drakonian?"

Alexis shook her head, "I don't know if they are Drakonian or not. They all looked like large human men to me. I didn't see any dragons in my brief vision." She stopped and thought for a moment. "I saw at least a dozen lined up to enter the ship, but I couldn't tell you if there were more already inside or not." She sighed, "I'm not being much help, am I?"

Ladon gave her a squeeze. "You are doing fine. We know they are coming and we know we will be considerably outnumbered. That gives us a starting point."

Ryuu stopped the sled so they could feed the dogs and give them an hour or so of rest. Everyone agreed that from this point on they would push straight through until they reached the Drakonian research facility.

"Are you sure this is where the facility is?"

Alexis looked around. In all directions, there was nothing but a sea of white. Not even mountains were there to break up the desolate landscape. The colors of the dancing aurora reflected off the sparkling ice expanse.

Ryuu consulted the satellite GPS device they had brought with them.

"These are the correct coordinates. If

Tugarin is still in stasis, it is possible that the entrance is buried in the glacier."

Ryuu pulled another device from the packs they brought with them on the plane. It was a crystal cylinder about the size of a man's palm. When Ryuu concentrated on the device, it began to glow a faint blue color.

"What is that?" Alexis asked.

Ladon answered, "It's a nano tracker. Normally it would be tuned to a certain dragon's nano machines so we could use it to locate them. They were used in combat to find missing soldiers or to track criminals once their whereabouts were traced to a specific geographic area."

"Then don't you need Tugarin's frequencies to find him?" Alexis questioned.

Ryuu shrugged. "Possibly, but I have set this thing to find any nano machines except for the three of us. So hopefully it will lead us to the research facility."

Ryuu started spiraling further and further out from the dog sled. Alexis watched him as she bounced, trying to keep her body temperature up. Ladon had said that her nanos could regulate her temperature, but all her small reserves of energy were being utilized to keep Fafnir out of her mind. The dragon was pushing harder and harder against her defenses. If they couldn't sever his connection soon, Alexis was going to go insane.

Suddenly Ryuu stopped about a hundred yards away from the sled and called Ladon and Alexis over. His tracker was blinking bright red.

"I think the entrance is below this ice somewhere." Ryuu grinned at his success.

"That's nice and all, but unless you somehow packed some heavy equipment into that small sled, how are we going to get through this massive sheet of ice?"

Both Ryuu and Ladon laughed at loud.

"You are still thinking in human terms, Alexis." Ladon gave her a squeeze. "I'm a fire dragon, remember?"

He stepped away from Alexis and started stripping. Ladon handed her his bundle of clothes as she marveled at the fact that he didn't even have goose bumps from the cold. Her eyes briefly drifted down…damn! No shrinkage either.

"Ryuu, take Alexis back to the sled team. I

have no idea how the dogs will react when I transform. Hopefully they won't take off since I should smell the same in either form, but you never know how an animal will react to a massive fire."

Ladon transformed into the massive red dragon Alexis first found in Wales. His jewel-like hide sparkled in the colors of the night. He really was a beautiful piece of art in this form. When she and Ryuu reached the sled team, Alexis sat in the sled to watch Ladon.

Ladon flapped his massive wings to hover in the air a few meters above the frozen ground. The red dragon gave a loud bellow, and the dogs started howling. The cacophony was deafening. Ryuu finally got the team back under control as Ladon opened his mouth wide. Alexis could see the air shimmering around Ladon's mouth as the temperature began to rise.

She had expected to see flames licking the ground, but there was no visible flame. The air just shimmered like the mirage of heat over the desert sands and the ice on the ground turned to steam almost instantly. Alexis couldn't see anything but the shadowed silhouette of Ladon hovering in the warm mist.

Melting through a glacier turned out to be a

rather monotonous task. Hollywood magic often made such ventures seem instantaneous, but the reality was Ladon had to take several breaks to let the steam disperse and to recharge his nanos with food. After several hours, Ladon finally called them over.

Nearly a hundred yards down in the glacier, a metallic door appeared. Ladon had graciously sloped the cuts into the ice so they could travel down on the dog sled. It was a good thing that the dogs were used to crossing frozen rivers and lakes, as the newly cut entrance had almost a mirror finish.

Ladon redressed and climbed into the sled next to Alexis. It was slow going because of the dangerously slick surface. A few of the dogs lost purchase on the slippery ice and would have continued to slide if they hadn't been tied into their harness.

At the end of the tunnel, Ryuu applied the brake on the sled, but they didn't stop. Ryuu pulled the leads on the dogs until they were sliding perpendicular to the metal door. A couple of dogs yelped in pain as they slammed against the metal wall of the facility. The sled was jerked hard enough that it tipped to one side, hitting the wall runners first. The impact jarred every bone in Alexis body, but nothing seemed to be damaged. The same couldn't be said for the sled.

Ryuu was the first to recover, since he had rolled away from the crashing sled. He went down the line to examine the dogs and remove them from their harnesses. Ladon helped Alexis up after he crawled out of the sled. Alexis looked down. The sled was mostly intact, but the runners had buckled and broken at impact. They wouldn't be using it to get out of here anytime soon.

"A few of the dogs have some scrapes and sprains, but as far as I can tell, no broken bones." Ryuu joined the pair.

Alexis looked at the sealed door. "Okay, what now?"

Ladon smiled as he walked towards the door. "This is the easy part." He laid his hand on a section near the door and closed his eyes. In a matter of moments, different circuits lit up, and the pressurized door disengaged with a hiss and quietly slid open.

"There are benefits to being an Imperial Hunter."

Ladon led while Ryuu took up the rear. Alexis knew the men put her in the middle for her protection, but looking around the facility, she wasn't sure it was needed. It had the same feeling of abandonment that Ladon's complex had when she had discovered it. The difference here was that instead of stone, she was surrounded by a metal substance that was curiously free from corrosion.

Their steps echoed along the long corridor. As they passed, the facility started to come to life. Evidently Ladon had sent his nanos slightly ahead of them. After a while Ladon stopped at a console. He tapped a few controls.

"Computer, scan for Drakonian life signs." He spoke in English for Alexis's benefit. In that moment Ladon sounded very much like the general he had once been. The longer Alexis was around Ladon, the more complicated the man became.

"Four sets of active nanos detected," The computer replied in monotone English.

Alexis frowned. That number didn't sound right.

"Display locations," Ladon barked.

A projected image of the facility schematic appeared in front of the console. On the display, three blips were clustered close together, while deep in the structure a lone blip appeared.

"Let's go." Ladon turned and marched off before Alexis could question anything. If anyone had been here, there should have been two Drakonian life signs; Tugarin and his mate Zoya. The fact that there was only one was disturbing. So many scenarios ran through Alexis's mind. Her companions had obviously already gone to the worst-case scenario because they tightened their guard around her.

The trio moved in silence as the lights blinked on slightly ahead of them. They came to a door that didn't automatically open for them. Ladon had to use an emergency override code to get in. They stepped into a space that had obviously been a living area at one time.

Alexis ran her hand along a dust-covered side table. The hand-carved wood seemed strangely comfortable placed against the metallic wall. She picked up a hunk of crystal and nearly dropped it when the image of a handsome, scholarly looking man with his arm wrapped around a petite blonde beauty appeared. Alexis knew without asking that this was an image of Tugarin and Zoya. She could also tell the pair was deeply in love. They had eyes only for each other and ignored the individual taking the picture entirely.

That look, there in that image, was what every woman dreamed about finding. It was the look that had sold centuries of romance stories, made billions for the entertainment industry. Alexis was beginning to hope that the Drakonian they found was some lab assistant or invader.

The group ventured further into the living space until they came to what was obviously a

sleeping chamber. What they found broke Alexis's heart. Centered on a large bed was the statue-like form of a sleeping blue dragon. Pinned under the front leg with its wings wrapped protectively around her was the mummified remains of a woman.

Amazingly, the beautiful gown she wore was still mostly intact. Her blonde hair still lay in a halo around her head. Her arms were wrapped lovingly around the massive fore leg of the dragon cradling her.

Tears rolled down Alexis's cheeks. "Dear god, Ladon…."

Ladon wrapped an arm protectively around Alexis. Everyone understood that even though Zoya's death had happened eons ago, the dragon sleeping next to her would wake for the first time to face a world without his mate.

"It seems cruel to wake him now," Alexis whispered. "Maybe we should just let him sleep."

Ladon hugged her close and she heard Ryuu sigh.

"It's too late now. As soon as we started disturbing this area in earnest, the process of him waking was already started."

Even as Ryuu spoke, the blue dragon's wing twitched.

"Ryuu, take Alexis to one of the common rooms," Ladon ordered.

Without a word, Ryuu started to take Alexis out of the room.

"Wait. Why do you want me to leave?" Alexis tried to reach out for Ladon as Ryuu pulled her along.

Ladon reached up and gently caressed Alexis's cheek. "Please, just go for a bit."

Alexis wanted to argue, but the deep sadness in Ladon's eyes made her just nod and follow Ryuu out. She watched Ladon until the door closed between them. Her last image before the door shut was Ladon walking towards the bed with slumped shoulders.

Alexis's heart stuttered and she wanted to run back to Ladon, just so he didn't have to face the difficult task of conveying Zoya's death alone, but Ryuu continued to pull her out of the living quarters and down the hall.

If it were just me, I would want you beside me to face this grave news, Ladon's voice whispered through her mind as he accessed the nanos that connected them. *But this will be painful for Tugarin and I think you being there when he wakes would hurt more than help.*

Alexis had to concede that Ladon was right, so she quit struggling against Ryuu and pushed her own feelings aside. This wasn't about her. It wasn't about Ladon. Alexis realized just how compassionate Ladon could be. While she had struggled against Ryuu and Ladon's request to get her way because of her own feelings, Ladon had set aside what he felt and wanted for Tugarin. It shamed Alexis to realize that she hadn't considered the blue dragon at all, just her own feelings and Ladon's.

Ladon let go of his connection to Alexis. He knew that if something were to happen with Alexis that he would go mad with grief. He had seen Tugarin and Zoya in life. Ladon knew that Tugarin's feelings for Zoya were no less intense than his for Alexis. It was possible that that Tugarin's feelings ran even deeper since he had spent many years living happily with Zoya.

Ladon wanted to give the blue dragon some privacy to grieve, but at the same time, he felt the

need to be there to make sure that the Tugarin didn't do something horrible in his grief. It was selfish, but they needed his scientific expertise.

The body of the blue dragon slowly came back to life. Bright blue jeweled eyes opened. Briefly, Tugarin's eyes reminded Ladon of Alexis's. When the blue dragon's eyes opened fully, he shimmered and shifted back to the form of a man, his arms still wrapped around Zoya's body.

Tugarin gently brushed his fingers over Zoya's hair, and her bones crumbled to dust. It was as if she had stayed whole just to give Tugarin a last goodbye. Ladon couldn't keep the tears from his eyes as he watched the man he once considered a friend fall apart.

Tugarin screamed out his anguish as he tried to piece Zoya's body back together, but each bone his lifted crumbled more with each touch. The inhuman sound that echoed through the rooms ripped at Ladon's soul. It made him wonder if they were going to lose Tugarin to the madness of his grief. There was nothing left to anchor him to this world.

Tugarin spotted Ladon across the room. His eyes turned feral and he growled a warning before launching himself at Ladon. Tugarin partially transformed, a gift few could master, and slashed

269

across Ladon's chest. Ladon didn't want to hurt his friend, so he only defended himself instead of attacking.

"Tugarin, it's me…Ladon."

No spark of recognition. Tugarin was lost in the pain and anger of his grief. Ladon wracked his brain trying to figure out a way to shake Tugarin free of his madness.

Then he remembered the eyes, how Tugarin's eyes reminded him of Alexis's. He remembered that Zoya and Tugarin had given birth to a couple children, one of which had amazingly been female, a miracle at the time when Drakonians almost exclusively produced males, hence the genetic colonies with other species. Ladon didn't remember what happened to the female offspring, and a connection to Alexis was a long shot, but if there was a connection, it might bring Tugarin out of his madness to know that something of Zoya remained in the world.

Alexis, have Ryuu compare your DNA to that of Tugarin and Zoya's.

Why? What is going on? I can feel that you are in pain.

Please just do it.

Ladon felt the connection close, and he hoped that the stubborn Alexis had relayed his request to Ryuu. The scan would only take a few minutes since bloodlines were so important to the Drakonians. But a few minutes would feel like a lifetime when battling for your life, especially if you weren't trying to kill the opponent that was trying to kill you.

Ladon dived behind a piece of furniture and rolled to another piece before Tugarin could see what he was doing. If he could get behind the blue dragon, he might be able to pin him down. Tugarin was stronger than any human male because he was Drakonian, but he was a scientist where Ladon was a warrior. Ladon had training and experience on his side.

Tugarin threw aside the couch that Ladon had originally dove behind. He was frantically searching, his appearance monstrous, with clawed hands and wings attached to a human-looking body. His teeth were sharp and elongated, the very vision of a demon from hell. The partial shift not only changed his appearance, but gave added strength to Tugarin. Ladon would need to partially shift himself to overpower his friend. The living quarters weren't large enough for two fully shifted dragons, so Ladon would have to subdue him quickly.

Ladon launched himself at Tugarin's back while the blue dragon searched for him. He shifted midair, adding a bit more bulk in addition to claws and wings. He hit Tugarin like a freight train and took the blue dragon to the ground.

The blue dragon started to shift.

"Don't," hissed Ladon.

Tugarin continued to fight Ladon's hold, adding size little by little, trying to tip the balance in his favor.

How did you know, Ladon?

Alexis's words slammed into his head. She really needed to work on control.

Doesn't matter, but I will tell you later. I need you to reach out to Tugarin and calm him down.

I don't have a connection to Tugarin. How can I contact him?

You are of the same bloodline. You have a connection; you just need to find it.

Alexis severed the connection once again and Ladon returned his focus to keeping Tugarin under control.

"Zoya?"

Ladon heard the question in Tugarin's voice, and he had to assume that Alexis had made her connection.

"I'm sorry my friend, but that is not Zoya. That is my mate, Alexis. She is of your bloodline, and she is beautiful."

Tugarin still struggled, but his movements weren't as insistent as before. Ladon could tell he was distracted. Alexis must still be communicating with him. Ladon decided to add his own arguments to whatever Alexis was telling him.

"Alexis is proof that Zoya lived and you loved each other. But my mate is in danger." Ladon heard Tugarin growl at that statement. Good, the blue dragon was feeling protective towards Alexis. "I need your help to keep her safe."

The fight finally left the blue dragon, and his body returned fully to that of a man.

Ladon could feel his friend sigh heavily. "I will listen to what you have to say. I would like to meet the woman who carries Zoya's voice. Now could you please get off me. You were always a heavy bastard."

Ladon gave a slight chuckle but rolled off Tugarin while returning to a man himself.

"Just so you know, I'm not sure that you are good enough for a female of my line," Tugarin stated while sitting up.

Ladon stood and extended a hand to his old friend. "No one would ever be good enough for Alexis. But no one will ever love her more than I do."

Tugarin took the proffered hand and stood. "I know that feeling well." He slapped Ladon on the back and started walking towards the door of the living quarters. "Let me meet my progeny to give me hope while I plan Zoya's funeral."

Alexis looked up at the scholarly man who walked into the common room with Ladon. Her connection to him was still new and disconcertingly strong. Ryuu tried to explain that it was because she was a direct descendent of Tugarin, but it still felt invasive, especially at the deluge of emotions she felt from him.

He loved his wife very much. His grief was a living breathing thing within him. Alexis didn't understand how he could function with the intensity of his emotions beating at him, but he appeared calm and composed as he walked towards her.

Tugarin extended his hand and Alexis instinctively took it. He searched her face as if looking for something. Alexis almost felt like she was being tested. She lifted her chin and waited for Tugarin to pass judgement on her; it was the only thing she could do given the circumstances.

"You have my eyes, but I can see my Zoya in the stubborn tilt of your chin, my dear." Tugarin gave a fatherly caress to Alexis's curls before pulling his hand away. "I am glad to know that something of her remains in the world."

Alexis took Tugarin's hand and gave it a squeeze. "Whether I was here or not, as long as you are in the world, a part of her is too."

Tugarin's eyes widened slightly, his mouth imitating a fish out of water until he smiled slightly.

"You are correct, little one. I will never forget my beloved Zoya."

Tugarin took a seat and waved at Ladon to do the same.

Everyone sat in silence for a while, no one knowing where to begin to sort out everything.

Finally, the silence became too much for Alexis and she addressed the elephant in the room.

"If Zoya was your mate, why didn't she fall into stasis like the rest of the Drakonians here on Earth?"

Three sets of male eyes shot to Alexis's face with varying degrees of shock, which turned to contemplation.

"Alexis is correct," Ryuu said. "We know that Zoya had gone through the transformation. Her nano machines were well established within her system. She should have fallen into stasis at the same time you did, Tugarin."

Alexis watched as Tugarin's eyes flicked back and forth as if he were scanning through a mental filing system. Then his eyes narrowed as he frowned. Suddenly the blue dragon jumped up with a string of what Alexis assumed were curses in a language she had never heard before. Alexis's breath began to fog as the temperature in the common room dropped dramatically.

"Control your nanos, Tugarin. Alexis is newly mated and has not learned control of her own nanos yet. I would take it very badly if you were to freeze my mate," Ladon growled.

"If the man wasn't dead by now, I would kill him myself," Tugarin hissed as he turned towards the rest of the company. "His stupid experiments cost my mate her life."

Understanding seemed to dawn on Ryuu and Ladon, but Alexis still didn't follow.

"What experiments? Who?"

Ladon took her hand, his thumb tracing circles on her palm. "You remember how we told you that Fafnir was exiled here?"

"Yes. You ultimately had the imperial guard come for him because he was of the royal bloodline but he was conducting horrible experiments on the population of this planet."

Ladon nodded, "And that was true…just not the whole truth."

Alexis frowned as Ladon hesitated. It was Tugarin that continued the explanation. "If Fafnir had confined his experiments to the human population, the Emperor would have never intervened."

Alexis gasped.

Tugarin sighed and continued, "The empire

viewed humans as useful for breeding, but they were not Drakonians. Only the few who had mated and went through the transition to become Drakonian had any rights, but even those were simply extensions of their male's rights."

"So you are saying that I am a second-class citizen in your *enlightened* civilization?" None of the men could miss the bite in Alexis's words.

"You are not a second-class anything," Ladon vehemently stated. "We don't even know the state of the empire now."

"Broken…it's broken," Alexis mumbled as she rubbed her temple. She had thought that her headache was simply lack of sleep and the strain of communicating with Ladon and Tugarin. But she could now feel the familiar rage of the ancient white dragon as he beat against her mental defenses.

Ladon saw the pain in Alexis's eyes and immediately was next to her trying to massage the tension from her shoulders.

"What is she talking about?" Tugarin asked Ryuu.

The black dragon heaved a sigh and set down the mug of tea he had made before Tugarin and

Ladon had walked into the room.

"Somehow Fafnir still lives. Or at least we think he does." Ryuu glanced over at Alexis, frowning at her obvious pain. "Neither Ladon nor I can feel him, but Alexis is somehow connected to him. It started during her transformation, and now that Fafnir is aware of the connection, he attacks her mind relentlessly, at one point even taking over her body to threaten Ladon. She hasn't slept in days because she can't keep him out when she dreams." Ryuu ran a hand through his hair, pulling at it in frustration. "It is killing her and I don't know how to stop it."

"The bastard did it." Tugarin fell back against his seat, shock and awe filling his expression. "I can't believe he did it."

"You obviously know something that we don't and we must discuss it soon," Ladon turned hard eyes on Tugarin. "But Alexis is the priority now. Can you get Fafnir out of her mind? Keeping him at bay is killing her slowly."

Tugarin really looked at Alexis for the first time. Pain edged her mouth as she clenched her jaw. Dark circles stood in deep contrast to the sickly pale complexion of her skin. Her hands trembled as she tried to lift the cup of tea to her lips. He sent his nanos out to assess just how bad it was. He was careful to stay out of her mind, not sure what the added strain of a second invader would be.

Tugarin's nanos were somewhat unique in that he could use them as a medical diagnostic tool. It was one of the primary reasons that Ladon had requested Tugarin be sent with the garrison stationed on Earth so many years ago. Until Fafnir had been exiled to Earth, Tugarin's deployment to Earth had been relatively peaceful. It allowed him to research the nano machines which despite generations of codependence his people didn't understand much about. It was Tugarin's research that Fafnir had based his own ideas on. But where Tugarin wanted to discover connections to the past, Fafnir wanted to control the future.

Tugarin closed his eyes as data flowed into his mind. Ladon hadn't exaggerated when he said this was killing Alexis. She still hadn't fully recovered from her transition, but despite the state of her physical body her nanos were going strong. The only thing keeping her functioning were the tireless machines that were repairing cells as they were breaking down, but the cycle of repair couldn't be sustained. If Alexis was unable to rest and recover soon, she would run out of both energy and material for her nanos to keep her body going.

Following a hunch, Tugarin examined Alexis's DNA and encoded into the mitochondrial was the strains of the virus that Fafnir had used on Zoya and their children. That virus had help to reprogram the nanos within their host. It had severed his mental connection to his mate since they were not blood related. It had dimmed the connection between him and is offspring. This was the first step in Fafnir's master plan.

Fafnir had observed that the patriarchs of certain bloodlines seemed to live considerably longer than others. He also noted that there was a correlation between times of illness for those elders and the deaths of the weaker members of the bloodline. It seemed to be a wasting illness that none of their scientists could find a cause for. The patriarchs seemed to find renewed vigor when their progeny died. Fafnir theorized that somehow the patriarchs used the life force of their progeny to extend their life. He was certain that it all related to the nanos machines.

When Fafnir approached Tugarin with his theories, Tugarin was extremely excited at first. He thought that they would discover a way to counter the wasting illness that others could do nothing about; but Tugarin quickly realized that Fafnir just wanted to find a way to immortality.

Tugarin couldn't remove the royal from his laboratory because he was after all a member of the royal bloodline. He tried to distance himself as much as he could from Fafnir. His avoidance was probably one of the reasons that he hadn't noticed what the white dragon was doing until it was too late.

Fafnir had made a few discoveries in his research and was able to introduce a virus that severed the familial connection between a bloodline's nano machines. It was how his connection to Zoya was severed. He then introduced a second virus to reprogram the nanos and connecting them to Fafnir.

It took the death of one of Tugarin's children that served as the catalyst needed to get the emperor involved. Fafnir literally sucked the life out of the child through the nano machines. This caused Tugarin to turn his considerable skill and knowledge to creating his own means of reprogramming the nanos. His method wasn't perfect. It didn't rest the nano machines back to their original configuration, but it locked Fafnir out. He had been forced to use his imperfect cure when Zoya started fading from the wasting sickness. It saved her life, but in the end Fafnir had his revenge as she died slowly, pinned next to the stasis frozen dragon that was her mate.

Her own nanos unable to shut down without the connection to Tugarin's.

Tugarin was jolted out of his memories when Alexis screamed. She clutched her head and doubled over. Fafnir was renewing his attacks and had evidently decided not to wait until she fell into an exhausted sleep to infiltrate her mind.

"They're here…in the solar system," she whispered through clenched teeth. "You have to let me leave. I'm the only one he can track." Alexis then collapsed.

Ladon gathered Alexis up in his arms and held her close, "Not a chance…stand or fall, we do it together." It didn't matter that Alexis probably didn't hear him.

Perhaps the brash general was the right mate for Alexis after all. Tugarin stood and motioned for the rest to follow.

"That bastard isn't taking any more of my family from me." Tugarin moved quickly through the corridors with Ladon carrying Alexis behind him. Blood was starting to trickle from Alexis's nose and Tugarin knew that even if he could introduce the new protocol into Alexis nanos that there was the possibility they could lose her.

Tugarin shook his head. They didn't have time for what ifs. They did nothing Fafnir's attacks would definitely kill her. A slim chance was better than none.

Alexis couldn't do anything but fight to remain conscious. She was vaguely aware that Ladon was carrying her someplace, but she didn't have the energy to focus on what was going on around here. Fafnir was beating at her mind, trying to pinpoint her location. He was draining energy from her nanos faster that she could boot up new ones. Her mind translated the nano battle as a fortress with a hundred white dragons attacking the walls. Each brick the dragon ripped free the soldiers who were the nanos under her control replaced, but she could see that the stores of bricks were dwindling and her soldiers were moving at a slower pace.

As more and more bricks fell under the claws of the white dragons, Alexis could see more and more of Fafnir's mind. He wanted her exact location. He wanted to know exactly how many Drakonians he didn't have under his control. Despite the rage and demands, Alexis could also feel the fear that everything was starting to fall apart. Fafnir was losing his mind to the paranoia that he would suffer the same fate as his predecessors. He was terrified of death.

Ladon set Alexis onto a cold metal exam table. She wanted to protest and tell him to at least warm it up first but she didn't have the energy to speak up. Her walls were starting to crumble.

She closed her eyes. She needed to rest, but soon a pair of hands were patting her cheeks and a voice was demanding that she open her eyes. Her lids felt so heavy, but at the demand in the voice she slowly forced them open.

Ladon's golden gaze stared back at her. She must be in really bad shape because she had never seen him look so afraid. She wanted to raise a hand to is cheek and comfort him, but she couldn't make her body work. She knew then that she was probably dying. Alexis's only regret was that she hadn't told Ladon how much she loved him.

Love?! Love is a fantasy. Use or be used. Attachments are weakness. You should give up and die, you weak woman. Your death will be the weapon I need to destroy Ladon for good.

Alexis heard the hissing voice in her mind. The blind rage that surrounded it let her know that it was the voice of Fafnir. She still had enough of her defenses to keep him from taking over her body, but she was fading fast until he threatened Ladon. That became a talisman to Alexis's heart and soul. She might not have the energy to save herself but she will find the energy to save Ladon.

The soldiers of Alexis's mind patched every hole in her fortress walls, giving her a brief reprieve from Fafnir. She was finally able to focus on the voices around her.

"I can sever Fafnir's connection to you, Alexis," Tugarin stated grimly. "But it is dangerous in your weakened state and will hurt like hell if you are conscious. I'm not Fafnir. I won't do anything without your consent."

"Please…this is killing you, Alexis." Tears flowed down Ladon's cheek.

Alexis raised a weak and trembling hand to Ladon's cheek and then turned her eyes towards Tugarin.

In a slurred voice, she said, "Can't be any worse than that monster in my head." She took a deep breath and said as she closed her eyes, "Just do it."

Tugarin wasted no time. He had Ladon lay Alexis flat on the table. He used his nanos to connect to the lab equipment. Consoles and machines flared to life. Soon the sounds of equipment whirring and monitors beeping filled the air.

Ladon and Ryuu stepped away and watched the medical ballet. They felt helpless, but knew that this was one task in which they couldn't help.

It didn't take long before a cover descended from the ceiling. It encased Alexis in a metallic coffin with only her face visible through a view screen. In that moment Ladon's heart stuttered because she looked dead, like she was laid out for a funeral. Ryuu pulled Ladon back as he tried to rush to Alexis's side.

"Normally I would introduce this virus in small doses, reprogramming the nanos in stages."

Tugarin was speaking to the men as he prepared. "However, he is already starting to drain the life out of her and he is using her as a beacon to find us. So, I am going to try a full system reboot."

Tugarin stopped and leveled an intense look on Ladon. "I have no idea how this is going to affect her, but I do know that it will be violent on her system."

Ladon's voice broke when he spoke, "He's already killing her. What choice do we have?"

Tugarin nodded and returned to his preparations. None of the men spoke. There was nothing more to say. This either worked or they would lose Alexis. With Fafnir's soldiers in the solar system, they had maybe a day to prepare. It would be simple for them to search for active nanos once they reached orbit. It wasn't like the days of old when Drakonians roamed all over the Earth.

"Alright." Tugarin's hand was poised over the control that would inject the virus into Alexis's system. The medical chamber he had sealed her in was programmed to force the virus to replicate at an insane rate.

With a nod from Ladon, Tugarin hit the button. For a moment, nothing seemed to happen, then Alexis's body started to convulse wildly. The seizures were so severe that the men were afraid she would injure herself within the medical chamber. Tugarin quickly ordered the chamber to strap her down as the convulsions continued.

Blood trickled out of Alexis's nose and ears.

"Her nanos can't handle the damage as Fafnir battles to keep them from being reprogrammed. We are going to lose her without nanos to repair her system." Tugarin was frantically hitting controls and watching the monitors.

"Lift the medical chamber," Ladon demanded. Tugarin looked at him confused for a second before the knowledge of Ladon's intentions dawned.

Quickly Tugarin raised the medical chamber and Ladon ripped open his clothes and tore away Alexi's clothes until he could expose as much skin as the straps holding her down would allow. He climbed on top of her, touching skin to skin wherever possible. He closed his eyes and concentrated. He sent an army of is nanos out towards his mate. The nanos protested the mass exodus but Ladon forced them to his will.

Soon Alexis's bleeding stopped and her vitals

stabilized. Tugarin caught Ladon as he lost consciousness and fell from the table. He quickly checked to see if the fire dragon was going to be alright and he could already sense the nanos returning to their master, their task completed.

Tugarin sank to the floor with Ladon's dead weight and he smiled. Then he started laughing. It was a hysterical laugh of relief.

Ryuu stared at the scientist, worried that the experiences of the last few hours had broken his mind.

Tugarin slowly regained his control and gently laid Ladon flat on the ground. Before standing. He checked a few monitors just to confirm what he knew before turning to Ryuu with a grin.

"We did it."

Ladon cracked his eyes open and even the dim light of the med-bed made his head hurt. It took him a moment to clear the fogginess from his mind.

He bolted upright, "Alexis!"

The world spun before his eyes making his stomach lurch. He fell back onto the bed with a groan. He heard a chuckle from the shadows off to his right and turned his head. The chuckle abruptly stopped when Ladon turned green at the movement.

Ryuu emerged from the shadows holding a bucket which Ladon promptly used to empty the contents of his stomach into.

"Tugarin said you would probably feel worse for wear after what you did for Alexis."

Ladon turned his eyes up to Ryuu, the question obvious in them, as he heaved again.

"Alexis is going to be fine, Ladon." He handed a damp cloth to Ladon. "She's sleeping in the next room over. Tugarin is monitoring her, just in case; but we severed Fafnir's connection. But her body needs rest, she was at her limit."

Ladon fell back against the bed. He felt surprisingly better now. "Have you been able to locate the Drakonians Alexis said were in the solar system?"

Ryuu sighed, "We have discovered an ion trail that indicates a ship has passed recently. The mathematical projections of their trajectory have them heading for Earth, but we haven't been able to pinpoint the ship."

Ladon struggled to sit up. He had to get out of bed. Ryuu and Tugarin were both intelligent and capable men, but they were scholars not soldiers.

Battle was Ladon's area of expertise.

"How far were you able to trace the ion trail?" Ladon questioned.

"It faded off around the planet the humans refer to as Saturn."

Ladon stood from the bed. He closed his eyes and took a deep breath. "It's been a few thousand years. I'm sure our tech here is antiquated compared to what Fafnir has available. But I remember a few theories that looked promising that have probably been developed now. See if you can pull up the research of Luo Fuxi. What you are describing sounds similar to something he was working on for the military."

"What are you going to do?" Ryuu said as he headed for the door.

"First, I'm going to check on Alexis. I need to see that she is okay with my own eyes. Then I am going to figure out how to keep her safe."

Ryuu left the room and Ladon was alone trying to get dressed. Several times he had to stop because the world tilted on its axis nearly causing him to fall over. He cursed his weakness. He couldn't afford to lay in bed recovering.

Best case scenario modern Drakonian ships weren't much faster than the ships he had once commanded. There was a limit to physics after all. But he was concerned that they hadn't picked the ships up on their monitors. Cloaking technology had just been an interesting theory when he had been in command. It appeared that it was no longer theory.

On the upside, Ladon knew that each new piece of tech came with advantages or disadvantages. He just needed an idea of this tech's weakness. Unfortunately, even if the ships weren't much faster than their predecessors that only gave them about forty-eight hours to prepare for an attack.

Ladon ran through various battle scenarios as he dressed. They would want a strongly defensible position away from the human populations. They needed to minimize not only exposure but collateral casualties as well.

That left their options primarily to be the research facility they were currently in or the Library island. This facility still had Drakonian technology that was functioning. It may be considered an antique now, yet it still was much more advanced than anything the humans had developed. The remote tundra kept humans away and unless Fafnir had sent another fire dragon, there was only one entrance in and out of the facility. In contrast the library, while remote, had no working tech and several points of access. More points than they had individuals to cover them, even if Alexis could fight with them.

Three dragons against a full squad, if Alexis's vision was correct. It wasn't completely hopeless, but it was steep odds. Ladon wiped a hand down his face. Defeat wasn't an option. He would never let Fafnir lay a hand on Alexis.

Ladon finally stood up fully dressed. Unlike the casual human clothes, he had ripped from him to help Alexis, he was now clothed in the typical uniform of a Drakonian soldier. He concentrated and connected his nanos to the tech in the battle suit. The nanos within the suit would now activate as various forms of armor during battle and retract to a small box affixed between his shoulder blades should he need to shift into his dragon form. It felt strange to be back in the role of soldier; but Ladon knew that it wouldn't take long before it felt natural to him once more.

*****

"How is she?" Ladon walked through the doorway before the door had fully slide out of the way.

He saw Tugarin gently brushing one of Alexis's stubborn curls from her face. Ladon buried his instinctual possessiveness at another dragon touching Alexis with such an intimate look. He had seen the storm of emotions Alexis had gleaned from Tugarin when he had sent his nanos to help heal her. He knew that the blue dragon had nearly been destroyed at the loss of Zoya. The only thing keeping him in this world was his connection to Alexis. As much as Ladon would love to keep Alexis only to himself, he couldn't in good conscious do that.

"She is recovering, but her body needs rest." Tugarin looks up at Ladon, his hand still laid gently on her brow. "Don't worry. I see her like a daughter, not as a replacement for Zoya."

Ladon walks into the room and sits in a chair on the other side of Alexis.

"I know," Ladon sighs.

Tugarin's lips quirk into a grin that doesn't quite reach his eyes, "Yeah, that growl must be something entirely different."

Ladon reaches for Alexis's hand. He concentrates as the nanos connect them. No nightmares, just a peaceful restorative sleep. He doesn't have the finesse to diagnose illness the way Tugarin can, but the nanos reassure him that she is indeed safe and recovering. The tension melts from his body finally. She wasn't going to die. They can sort out the rest later.

"I wouldn't trust the doctors when Zoya was ill or pregnant either. I always had to make certain myself." Tugarin looked down at Alexis and sighed. "They are too precious to take for granted." He leaned back in his chair, taking his hand from Alexis and looking Ladon over thoughtfully. "I've known you a long time Ladon and to be honest I wasn't sure you would be good for Alexis. You were a playboy with a violent streak." He raised a hand when Ladon stated to protest. "It made you a great soldier. But I saw Alexis's mind and memories when she reached for me. Her lack of experience and my despair made it a much deeper connection than either one of us was ready for. She needs a man, not a soldier. She needs a commitment that I wasn't sure you were capable of giving. You know just as well as I do that finding a true mate is intense, our genetics are compatible in an almost perfect harmony; but while our instincts push us to be together and our emotions get involved, a true mate pairing doesn't guarantee a good match between people."

Tugarin stopped and stared down at Alexis.

"I wasn't sure you would be capable of the commitment she would need to be happy. But then you went and did something stupid." Tugarin barked a laugh, "Love always makes you do something stupid." He looked up and stared Ladon in the eyes, "You could have died, Ladon. Pushing that many nanos into Alexis's body from your own could have killed you. If fact, we almost lost you. What were you thinking?"

Ladon looked away from Tugarin and stared at Alexis's face as if he was trying to memorize every contour. His thumb absently traced circled on the pulse of Alexis's wrist; it's steady beat reassuring him that all was well. "I wasn't thinking. All I knew was Alexis had to live."

Tugarin nodded and pushed up from his chair. "Then I leave her in your care with my blessing."

The blue dragon walked towards the door but was stopped by Ladon's voice. "She still needs you, you know."

Tugarin ducked his head and sighed, "I won't join Zoya yet. I have some unfinished business with Fafnir."

"I think we all do," Ladon responded. "Good

rest, my friend."

Tugarin slipped out of the room and Ladon turned his gaze back to Alexis. Her curl was once again covering her eyes and he gently brushed it out of the way with a smile. She was so beautiful, and he didn't mean just physically. She would have sacrificed her life to protect those that she cared about. She reached out to a raging dragon, that she didn't know, to bring him some comfort. Ladon knew that once she awoke she would do whatever she could to keep Tugarin here in this world and help his heart heal because she couldn't help bringing him into her circle of care. That was what was beautiful and magical about Alexis, everyone she encountered she would welcome into her care. It didn't matter if it was family, student, friend, or lover she had room in her heart for them all. Ladon had never known a being more capable of loving than Alexis.

It was his job to make sure that loving spirit stayed in this world and thrived. Tugarin was right about one thing, he was a soldier. He was comfortable with death and violence. As much as he longed for the peaceful life with Alexis, he would resurrect his skills to protect her if necessary.

The door opened with a swish. Ladon didn't even look up.

"I found some information on Luo Fuxi."
Ryuu popped his head into Alexis's medical room.

"Send it to the console in the common room.
I'll be there in a little while." Ladon stood and
placed a loving kiss on Alexis's forehead. She gave
a gentle smile at his touch even in her sleep. "Give
me about an hour then you and Tugarin need to meet
me. We have a battle to plan."

39

"Are you sure about this?" Tugarin looked over Ladon's shoulder to the console display. "Even if you are correct that tech will be at least a few centuries old if not eons."

Ladon punched a few keys running numbers through the simulator. "There is a limit on physics even if you improve the technology. I've run several simulations. Our enemy will be here in within the day."

"So we are staying here?" Ryuu asked.

"We don't have a choice. Alexis can't be moved." Ladon growled in annoyance. He had to keep reminding himself he wasn't dealing with soldiers, but the repeated questioning of his battle strategy was wearing on already frayed nerves.

If they didn't quit discussing and start preparing they were going to get caught with their pants down. They were already working at disadvantage.

"I really think…" Ryuu began.

Scales rippled across Ladon skin. He hadn't lost control like that since he was an adolescent.

Ladon's roar echoed across the facility. "Quit thinking and just do. Fuck…we would still be sitting here debating as the enemy crashes through our door." Ladon grabbed Ryuu by his shirt and pulled him up until they were standing nose to nose. "I will not your scholarly sensibilities endanger my mate. The time for debate has passed. If you want to survive the coming battle soldier up. Follow orders. MY orders."

Ryuu laid his hand over Ladon's fist. "Okay."

Ladon let Ryuu fall back into his seat and

turned on Tugarin. Tugarin just raised his hands. "You're the hunter. I concede to your expertise."

"Finally," Ladon threw his hands up and fell back into his chair. He pulled up a schematic of the facility and started laying out his defense strategy.

He sent Ryuu and Tugarin off to accomplish a series of tasks. Booby traps in the surrounding area as well as down the main corridor. Alexis was moved to a more secure location. The odds were not in their favor, but if they could funnel their attackers into the tight confines of the corridor then they had a chance of picking them off a few at a time and wearing them down. This was his Thermopylae. He would save Alexis even if he died in the process.

He had to figure out a way to put their ship out of commission. Ladon doubted that military strategy had changed all that much. Weapons and technology may change through the years, but at its core battle was about out maneuvering your opponent.

If Ladon had been assigned the mission he would only send out a portion of his men until he assessed the capabilities of the enemy. Especially if he had been under the impression that the enemy was just a woman and maybe a couple of other opponents. But Ladon wasn't just any opponent. He was one of the greatest battle generals of Drakonian history, even if Fafnir erased his name from their traditions, he could not erase the experience that shaped Ladon.

Ladon had been so successful against overwhelming odds in the past because he didn't rely on brute strength. He was an intelligent strategist, willing to use any and all knowledge at his disposal.

That was one of the reasons he was studying Luo Fuxi's theories. He was the father of Drakonian cloaking technology. Fuxi's work was new when Ladon was still an imperial soldier; but he was the only one who had been able to create a working cloaking mechanism. So, it stood to reason that everything since built on that foundation.

Unfortunately, the technobabble in the papers were giving Ladon a headache. He was about to put the thing away to take a break when he skimmed over a section. There...Ladon reread the section. Finally, he might have found a weakness.

*****

Ladon and Tugarin were modifying one of the planetary defense weapons that had been outfitted at each Drakonian facility. It wouldn't do them much good against a fleet, but as far as they knew they were only dealing with a single ship. All Drakonian ships were controlled via nano integration by the crew. There is little reason to think that had changed.

"Are you sure this is going to work?" Ladon continued entering the information Tugarin told him to input. It was a long and arduous process. "The virus you used on Alexis was biological in nature."

"All DNA is simply a code that tells proteins how to form which then connect to form something else and the process goes on until the organism is complete. Though one could argue that organisms connect through the life cycle and processes of life and death to form an entire planet, which connects to other planets to for the solar system. Which connects…"

"Okay, I get it. Hold the lecture until after the battle." Ladon chuckled. "Did you change the programming?"

"As requested this virus will sever the crew's connection to the ship; but aren't Drakonian ships protected against outside information being downloaded?"

"Normally but per Fuxi's research any ship using the cloaking technology is vulnerable when they drop the cloak to allow shuttles to exit."

"I think I remember that paper. He cloaked ships using what amounted to a vast cloud of nano machines whose job was to change sensor data surrounding the ship."

Ladon entered another line of code, "Exactly. And if they were working they couldn't be hacked; but they have to be shut down when a shuttle is launched from the main ship, otherwise the cloaking nanos can accidently cause malfunctions in the shuttle's systems."

"And while they are shut down they can be reprogrammed." Tugarin nodded. "It is a sound plan, but it will only work if the virus is ready for download when they get here."

Almost as soon as Tugarin made that last statement the orbital alarms started going off.

"You just had to jinx us," Ladon shouted over the alarm as he bolted from the console. "Finish the code. Be ready to launch it when they send the second wave of soldiers."

"Are you so sure they will send a second wave?"

"They will have to if the first wave is dead."

Ladon stopped by Alexis's room on the way
to his battle station. She was still sleeping
peacefully despite the alarm. Tugarin had given her
a sedative to ensure that her body got the rest it
needed. Ladon caressed her cheek and gave her a
gentle kiss. He set a series of traps near her door as
a last line of defense. Hopefully it wouldn't come to
that, but he wasn't taking chances.

He passed by Ryuu who was stationed in the
main corridor. The plan was Ladon would push the

soldiers to the tight confines of the corridor where Ryuu would pick them off. Once Tugarin disabled the ship, he would join Ryuu in defending the corridor while Ladon picked off stragglers from the rear. It was a solid plan, but it counted on being able to physically outlast the enemy. Ladon prayed that the other two men cared enough for Alexis to last.

Ladon active his nanos and his battle suit retracted. He opened the facility door and walked out into the burning cold naked. When he cleared the tunnel of ice, he transformed into his dragon and waited.

"Virus ready for upload." Tugarin's voice buzzed over the communication network.

In his dragon form Ladon had to use his nanos to communicate and sent instructions to monitor the orbit, especially near the last know location of the ship. As soon as another shuttle launched Tugarin was to send the virus.

Ladon's dragon vision caught a streak of light on the horizon. The human population would assume that a meteor had fallen, but Ladon knew that was the shuttle entering the atmosphere. They appeared to be landing at the human settlement where they had procured the sled dogs. Ladon prayed that the Drakonian soldiers left the humans alone, but he knew that was doubtful of men under Fafnir's command.

It took days to reach the research facility by dog sled; but Ladon and his group had been trying to stay hidden from the human authorities. The Drakonians sent after them wouldn't even consider staying hidden. In the shuttle, they could be at the facility in under an hour. In dragon form it would only be a matter of hours.

Ladon took the time waiting for the attack to build a makeshift fortress. He used his fire to melt the surrounding glacier ice. He used the wind from his wings to create tall walls of water and then used his nanos to manipulate the surrounding temperature of the water freezing the walls into a thick, sparkling dome of ice. Ladon may have an affinity for heat, but cold was just a lack of heat. Most people, even Drakonians, didn't consider that a nanos affinity for one aspect also allowed the person to manipulate that aspects opposite. It was essentially the same elements just different ends of the spectrum.

Ladon had just finished the domed fortress when he saw the glint of the metallic shuttle on the horizon. The battle was about to begin. He crouched behind the walls and waited as the shuttle landed about a hundred yards from the ice dome.

Ladon prepared for the attack. Surprisingly, the first assault was mental.

Ladon felt foreign nanos invade his mind as a half dozen soldiers poured out of the shuttle. The dragon was strong; but Ladon had defeated Fafnir in mental combat. He violently shoved the enemy out of his mind. He shut down and disposed of the enemies nanos, but not before sending a reverb of violence through the tiny machines. Ladon knew that his attack had hit its mark when one of the soldiers grabbed his head and stumbled.

One of the soldiers transformed. He was an orange dragon with black tips to his scales. The enemy braced himself on the other side of the ice dome and opened his great jaws to spray flame across the frozen fortress.

Ladon shook his head. The imperial army was sorely lacking in proper training. Instead of concentrating his flame to create an opening for his fellow soldiers, the dragon was wasting time trying to melt the entire fortress.

Disgusted, Ladon burst through the ice and flame and tackled the dragon to the ground. The enemy turned his flame on Ladon. Ladon didn't even register the attack as his nanos adjusted the temperature to prevent injury. Fafnir had sent these me to battle without any information on their enemy.

Ladon easily pinned the dragon to the ground. His jaws snapped the dragon's neck and he returned to his humanoid form as the energy in his nanos died out. Two of the remain five soldiers looked on in horror and fear as the other three scrambled through the opening Ladon had created when he attacked the dragon.

Ladon raised his head to the sky and bellowed his victory. The two remaining soldiers quickly transformed and attacked him together. Their attack was uncoordinated and ineffectual. It was like fighting new recruits. Neither dragon lasted long against an experienced warrior.

Ladon heard Ryuu through the communicators that a second shuttle had launched and the virus upload was successful. The ship was dead in orbit and the second shuttle had crash landed just a few miles away from the research facility.

On the horizon Ladon saw four more dragons winging swiftly towards him. He took to the sky and engaged them in aerial combat. Again, he was met with poorly trained soldiers. What had happened to the fierce armies of the Drakonian Empire?

He rose high into the sky and then tucked his

wings for a rapid dive at his enemies. His talons shredded one dragon's wings and the bulk of his body slammed into the back of a second. The impact broke the dragon's back and he too fell to the earth.

The two remaining dragons circled Ladon, careful to stay out of reach of his deadly claws. They actually tried to coordinate their attack. One dragon pulled water from the atmosphere as the other lowered the temperature to form ice on Ladon's wings. As attacks went it wasn't a bad one, but it showed that they hadn't studied their enemy. Ladon adjusted the temperature around him making the ice melt as soon as it touched his scales, reducing their attack to nothing more than a parlor trick.

Ladon attacked the water dragon who had crept closer to expend less energy in his water attack. Ladon's front claws latched on to the poor dragon holding him in place as his hind claws shredded the water dragon's stomach. Ladon raised high into the air and then turned to drop like a stone with his burden. As the ground quickly came closer he threw the injured dragon with all his might, shattering his head and ending his suffering.

The last dragon looked on in horror, realizing that all his comrades were dead. He turned tail and ran back towards the shuttle's crash site. Ladon was in pursuit when the dragon suddenly dropped from the sky. Ladon landed next to the body of his enemy. He had returned to the form of a man and blood poured from his nose, eyes, and ears. Ladon doubted that it was the impact that caused those bloody injuries. Evidently Fafnir despised cowards.

By this time Ladon was feeling almost insulted at what Fafnir had sent to battle him. He didn't bother to hurry after the three remaining soldiers. Ryuu and Tugarin could easily dispatch them. He did follow their battle plan and blocked off their route of escape; but he didn't remain in dragon form. It was an unnecessary expenditure of energy.

He passed the bodies of two of the enemy soldiers. When he rounded the corner, he found the third on his knees with Ryuu in front of him. This enemy was the only one to have a soldier's eyes. He didn't beg for his life. He only asked that his death be swift.

Ryuu raised his phase gun to deliver the death blow, but Ladon called out to him.

"Wait. We need information. Keep that one alive."

There was something troubling Ladon about this whole thing. A good hunter knows when he needs to gather intel.

"How many remain aboard the ship?"

Ladon paced in front of their prisoner. Despite being tied upright to a chair for almost twenty hours the man stayed resolutely silent. If this continued Ladon would have to do something he loathed; invade his mind. Ladon was an honorable man and even as a soldier he hated the use of torture to retrieve information. But sometimes it was necessary.

With a sigh Ladon pulled a chair directly in front of the man and sat down. If he had to resort to torture, it was only fair that Ladon remember this man's face.

"I wish you would talk to me. I'd rather not be cruel, but I will be if I must. I will do anything to keep those I love safe."

That statement seemed to catch the man's attention as he cocked his head to one side instead of staring blankly ahead.

Ladon leaned forward, "Do you have a mate? No? When you discover them, you will find that you will do anything for them. I will not let Fafnir have her and if that means I have to go through you to keep her safe I will."

The man tied to the chair shook his head. "You don't understand. Fafnir already has her. He can bleed her life force dry even from a distance once he is in her mind. He could use her to kill you and you would be none the wiser. We were only sent to retrieve her because she is strong. Fafnir wants to drain her slowly because he hasn't encountered nanos that powerful in centuries."

Ladon was taken aback by the hate in the man's voice, but he sensed it wasn't directed at him but rather Fafnir. "What is your name?"

"Cadmus."

"What if I told you, Cadmus, that we severed the connection Fafnir had?"

Cadmus's eyes took on a fever sheen. "That is not possible. Fafnir kills off anyone who even considers trying to find a way to break away from him."

Ladon just raised a brow and stood up. He walked to the door and laid his palm on the lock. The door disengaged with a hiss and slid open. Without another word, he closed the makeshift prison door behind him and went in search of Tugarin.

He found the blue dragon in Alexis's room. Ladon was happy to see Alexis was sitting up. Her color looked much better and she was laughing at something Tugarin had said to her.

"Ladon!" Alexis reached out for him.

Ladon took her hand and bent to place a kiss on her cheek. "How are you feeling?"

"Much better. It is amazing what sleep can do for a person." She searched his face and frowned. "Something is bothering you."

Ladon pulled up a chair to sit beside Alexis's bed. Tugarin stood to give the pair some privacy but

Ladon stopped him. "I want you to hear this too. In fact, get Ryuu."

Tugarin nodded and left to retrieve the black dragon, leaving Ladon and Alexis alone.

Ladon stared at their intertwined hands. "I'm sorry," He said softly.

"For what?" Alexis asked genuinely confused.

"For putting you through this. If I hadn't selfishly mated you, you wouldn't have had to go through nearly dying twice."

Alexis reached out and cupped his cheek, gently insisting he raise his head to look in her eyes. "I won't lie. In the beginning, I was afraid. But I wasn't afraid of Fafnir or the consequences of acquiring nano machines. I was afraid that it was just sex and passion between us." She laid a finger across his lips when he would speak. "God knows we burned hot in that department. But every man I would come to care about, didn't care about me in the same way even if they said they did." Alexis sighed, "I fell in love with you but a part of me thought that it wouldn't be possible for you to love me the same way." Alexis closed her eyes and gathered her thoughts. "I guess what I am trying to say is that I don't regret anything that has happened since we mated."

"How can you not regret it? Nightmare, constant mental attacks…Damn it! You nearly died when we severed the connection."

Alexis used both hands to grab his face and force him to look at her. "But you saved me. Don't you see, Ladon? No matter how much you loved me, I would always question it and I would have eventually pushed you away because I didn't trust you to actually love me. If you hadn't forced your nanos into me when I was dying, I would still be questioning it."

"I don't understand."

"I felt everything that time…. every thought, every emotion. I had undeniable proof of your love for me. It makes me a horrible and shallow person, but honestly it was what I needed to erase any doubts about us. We are going to fight and disagree. That is life. But now I won't be poisoning our relationship thinking of it as proof that I was right and you really didn't love me."

Ladon laid his forehead against hers. "For such a smart woman, you really can be an idiot."

"I know. For an ass, you can be really sweet."

"I know," Ladon said with a grin. He shifted his head just enough to capture Alexis's lips. The kiss quickly went from sweet to hungry.

"Dad, Ladon's kissing Alexis again," Ryuu called over to Tugarin in a tattling voice as the pair walked into the room. Ladon flipped the black dragon off and continued to kiss his mate.

Tugarin cleared his throat, "There was something you wanted to discuss with all of us?"

Ladon reluctantly ended his kiss with Alexis. He settled himself on the bed next to her wrapping her in the protection of his arms.

"Can the virus you used to sever Fafnir's connection Alexis be used on a born Drakonian?" Ladon asked.

"Most likely. Why?" Tugarin replied.

"I think we should use it on our prisoner."

"But you told me that if you couldn't get anything out of him voluntarily today that you would pull it forcibly from his mind." Ryuu interjected.

Alexis gasped, "I remember the pain of you invading my mind when we first met and that just lasted a few moments. That would basically amount to torture if you did it for a prolonged period."

Ladon acknowledged what Alexis stated with a nod. "Which is why I'd rather not resort to that if I didn't have to."

"What does any of this have to do with the virus?" Tugarin asked.

"Something has been bothering me about this entire attack. The soldiers sent to retrieve Alexis were reluctant and untrained. The only one that even seemed like a real warrior was Cadmus."

"Cadmus?" Alexis asked.

"That's the name of the dragon we captured." Ladon clarified. "As I was saying he was the only one with a warrior's eyes, but he easily surrendered and then begged for a swift death. None of them seemed like they actually wanted to be doing Fafnir's bidding."

"Or he could be playing a game to gather more information," Tugarin stated.

Ladon conceded that was a possibility. "But I have the feeling that he is at the mercy of Fafnir as much, if not more, than Alexis was."

"So you are hoping that severing Fafnir's control would gain you a knowledgeable ally." Alexis' shrugged. "It is a definite pro. My concern would be even if we sever the connection, would that be enough to break a lifetime of cultural norms. I got the impression that Fafnir has set himself up as some sort of all-knowing god king."

"Plus you said that you didn't want to torture the man if you didn't have to. You saw what the process did to Alexis. It could be much worse for him. He has been connected for a much longer time." Tugarin shook his head. "I don't know if this is a good idea."

Everyone fell silent, lost in their own thoughts for a moment.

"I think we should try it," Alexis finally spoke up. "If we sever the connection and he still turns out to be Fafnir's man then we do what Ladon planned to do in the first place. Nothing changes. But if he is here under duress like Ladon thinks he is, then freeing him from Fafnir puts him in our debt. We can use that."

"You know there is the possibility that Fafnir will just kill him off before we can finish the process," Tugarin states.

"Then we are in the same place we have always been and nothing has changed," Ladon responds.

"I'm not sure I like this. If we go around mucking with people's nanos without their consent what makes us any different from that bastard Fafnir?" Tugarin crosses his arms with a glare.

Alexis laid a hand on Tugarin's arm. "In an ideal world you are right. But this world is not ideal. This is war. I've had a lot of time to think about this as I battled to keep Fafnir out of my head. His connection has taken away the choice of an entire species. He is using it not only to control but to kill. Is it wrong to invade people's mind and body without permission? Yes. Am I willing to bear the burden of that necessary evil if it frees people? Yes."

Tugarin wiped a hand over his face with a sigh. "Finc. I'll help."

"Thank you," Alexis wrapped her arms around Tugarin and hugged him.

Cadmus's eyes narrowed as the group descended upon him in mass. They widened in surprise as Alexis stepped from behind Ladon.

"Get her out of here," Cadmus growled between clenched teeth. His eyes were shut tightly as if trying to remove the sight of Alexis from his mind.

Suddenly Cadmus's voice changed. "So you are alive, my dear. I had feared that my onslaught had killed you when the connection broke. But once again you prove formidable. I'm going to enjoy sucking you dry. Your nanos will sustain me for years to come. You should feel priv…"

Tugarin's fist fired out. It connected with Cadmus's jaw with an audible crack. The prisoner slumped in his chair unconscious. Alexis immediately closed her eyes and sent her nano machines rushing towards Cadmus's mind. She heard Ladon's protest when he realized what she was doing. It sounded far away even though she could feel him right beside her. She knew if they were going to be successful that this was necessary.

"I'm the only one who can hold Fafnir at bay," Her voice strained with effort. Already Fafnir was throwing his attacks at Alexis's protective wall. "Just get it done before we lose him."

Ladon picked Alexis up while Ryuu and Tugarin carried Cadmus. They quickly headed to the medical area. Ladon laid Alexis on one bed, but refused to let go of her hand. Cadmus was laid on the med table and was quickly covered by the device that Tugarin had used to deliver the virus to Alexis. Once again they were pushing the limits of a body to cut off Fafnir.

"Is this going to hurt Alexis?" Ladon asked

Tugarin.

"She already has the virus in her system so she shouldn't be bothered by a second exposure. Her nanos have already been reprogrammed, so she, in theory, should be fine."

"In theory?!" Ladon squeezed her hand.

"Just do it, quickly. Something has changed. Fafnir seems stronger for some reason. I don't know how much longer I can hold him off." Alexis rubbed her temple with her free hand.

With a few adjustments for the size of the new patient, Tugarin injected the virus in multiple places across Cadmus's body. For a moment, nothing happened. Then Cadmus started convulsing and Alexis started screaming.

Instinctually all three remaining males sent nanos out to assess what was happening with Alexis. Each saw what was happening differently. Ladon saw images of a metaphorical battle in his mind. Alexis was the avenging warrior woman protecting the innocent masses. Ryuu heard Alexis's voice as if from far away in his head telling him that Fafnir was trying to kill Cadmus and possibly her. Tugarin had the clearest picture as his nanos diagnostic ability allowed him to see her nanos trying to protect

Cadmus's nanos that had shut down to reprogram from the remaining nanos still under Fafnir's control.

The three men pushed nanos into Cadmus's system. They helped push back the Fafnir controlled nano machine. It soon became clear that while it would weaken Cadmus for a while the safest thing would be to physically destroy the remaining enemy nanos. Led by Alexis's nanos the others herded the enemy nanos into a single area. Unfortunately, Fafnir was smart enough to collect the nanos he controlled in the nervous system, specifically Cadmus's brain. If they weren't careful the destruction of the nanos that hadn't reprogrammed could cause permanent damage.

The group paused their onslaught, unsure what to do. They needed to save Cadmus, if they had any hope of finding out what the hell was truly going on. In the end their choice was taken from them.

Fafnir must have sensed that he was going to be defeated in this battle because the nanos he controlled started destroying Cadmus's brain tissue. The poor man's body jerked with violent seizures. The group couldn't hold back any longer and started to systematically destroy the occupied nanos.

It took nearly an hour as they chased the last

few down, but ultimately they removed the last of the Fafnir controlled nano machines, leaving Cadmus with a diminished number of nanos only under his own control.

They all pulled out, except for Tugarin; and Alexis collapsed against Ladon in exhaustion.

"We have got to figure out a better way to do this," Alexis panted. "I can't keep doing this for an entire race."

Ladon held her close and caressed her hair. He didn't say anything because he wasn't sure that there was another way to do this. That was a question for the researcher and the scholar.

"He's stabilized," Tugarin said as he finally pulled out of Cadmus. "There is brain damage, but we won't know the full extent until he wakes up. Hopefully over time as his remaining nanos build back up, they will eventually be able to repair the damage Fafnir caused."

"Go get some rest while you can. There is still a ship floating in orbit out there and no telling how many more Fafnir has dispatched." Ladon picked Alexis up to carry her to bed as he spoke to the others.

"I'll take first watch," Ryuu said. "Someone should keep an eye on our guest. I can monitor the orbit as well."

Ladon nodded and carried the sleeping Alexis to the guest quarters she had been using. He retracted his uniform and crawled into bed next to her, pulling her flush against his body. He vowed that one day soon she would be able to rest and recover. Maybe they would take a luxury vacation where their every whim was catered to. Or perhaps a secluded island with just the two of them would be better. Ladon fell asleep planning the vacation they both would need after this.

Alexis was sitting with Cadmus, the weapon
Ladon insisted on her having sitting on the table next
to her. She still had difficulty controlling the
information her nano machines glean when she sends
them into someone's mind. She tried to explain to
Ladon that she knew Cadmus was a good man and
the weapon wasn't necessary, but still he insisted.
She finally gave in to give him piece of mind.

A groan from the bed brought her attention
over to the patient. Cadmus's eyes fluttered until he
finally opened them, promptly shielding his eyes

from the light in the med room. Alexis dimmed the lights.

"How are you feeling?" she asked quietly.

"You shouldn't be here," Cadmus's speech was slightly slurred and Alexis noticed that the right side of his face dropped slightly.

"It's alright."

Cadmus tried to sit himself up in the bed. "No he could use me to get to you."

Despite his weakened state Cadmus tried to help her.

"Shhh," Alexis pushed him back down into the bed. "Search within yourself. Fafnir can't reach you anymore."

Cadmus let her lay him back down. He closed his eyes with a frown and turned his concentration inward. After a few moments, his eyes popped open.

"How?" Tears shimmered in Cadmus's eyes. "I'm free."

He settled back into the pillows and his eyes drifted down. Alexis knew from experience that he would be exhausted until he got a good night's rest.

"Where are the males?" He asked.

Ladon would probably be upset that she answered truthfully to a possible enemy; but Alexis knew that Cadmus was now theirs not Fafnir's. "They detected some activity from the ship. They had hoped it would remain dead in the water, so to speak, for a bit longer."

"No…" Cadmus struggled to a sitting position and swung his legs over the bed. Before Alexis could stop him, he tried to stand. His body was not only weak but the right side didn't respond as easily as he had expected and he fell to the ground.

Alexis got her small frame under an arm and struggled to help him stand. "You haven't recovered yet. You should stay in bed, especially with the trauma to your brain from expelling Fafnir."

She sat him on the edge of the bed and he grabbed her wrist with surprising strength.

"You don't understand. I need to talk to your mate," Cadmus's voice was urgent. "Now!"

Alexis shook her head and laid Cadmus back into bed. "Okay. I'll bring him to you."

"Hurry."

Alexis turned and ran out of the med room.

"Location of Ladon," she called as she ran down the hall.

The research facility responded with a mechanical voice. "Control room three."

"Direct me."

Lights began flashing along the wall and Alexis ran in the direction they indicated. She burst into the control room just a few minutes later.

"Alexis!" Ladon jumped up and rushed to her. "Is everything alright?"

Alexis was promising her inner monologue that they would be joining a gym in the near future between gasping breaths. She had always hated running.

"Cadmus needs to talk to you. When I told him that you detected movement from the ship…"

"You what?" Ladon growled.

Alexis waved a dismissive hand, "Chew my ass later. This is an emergency. Go talk to him, now."

"Sit!" Ladon barked at her as he pointed to a chair. He then turned and marched towards the med room.

When he opened the door, Cadmus groused at him.

"Took you long enough."

"Alexis said what you had to say was important so here I am," Ladon crossed his arms and glared at Cadmus.

Cadmus sighed, "I get that you don't trust me. I wouldn't in your shoes either. But I am trying to help."

"So help," Ladon took a chair across the room and sat.

"Our squad was a new formation. To be honest, my men and I were meant to only be cannon fodder while they prepared the real attack."

Ladon leaned forward, "I'm listening."

"You know that Fafnir likes to experiment, right?"

"And he doesn't care what happens to his experimental subjects either," Ladon nodded. "That hasn't changed in the eons since my last encounter with him."

"Yeah well, he has had centuries of unchallenged control over a huge population he could use as experimental subjects on a whim. In the last few decades he has been obsessive about creating the perfect soldier. Unfeeling, super strong, and ultimately loyal."

Ladon looked thoughtful, "You're saying some of these experiments are on board that ship, aren't you?"

"Not some...just one." Cadmus wiped sweat from his brow, inwardly cursing his own weakness. "Believe me, all it takes is one. The damn thing is a monster and almost impossible to kill. It is more nano tech than organic."

"So what are you suggesting we do?"

"Run...Just one of those things could lay waste to the majority of this planet."

"Fuck!" Ladon jumped up and started to pace. "I can't let something like that run amuck on this planet. Like it or not, this is our home. Not to mention the humans would be slaughtered."

Cadmus sighed, "I kind of figured you would

say that. But I had to give you my warning anyway." He laid back down and rolled over. "You broke Fafnir's hold on me; something no one else has been able to accomplish before dying. That is a miracle in my book. Maybe you have another miracle in there somewhere."

Ladon stopped his pacing and watched Cadmus's shoulders slump. He thought he heard the man say that at least he got to die free. With one last look, back at the man on the bed, Ladon walked out of the med room. He needed to talk to the others. He didn't believe in miracles, but he did believe that a good strategy could win despite overwhelming odds. It was time to come up with some plans.

Ladon was rushing towards the common room that the rest of the group was in. A great boom was heard and the earth shook, knocking Ladon to his knees. He stood and ran towards Alexis. He had to make sure she was safe. His reached out through the nanos that connected them and felt that she was startled but alive and she was getting closer.

Ryuu, Tugarin and Alexis met Ladon in the hall.

"Sensors spotted the main ship orbiting right above us." Tugarin said.

"Evidently they decided to attack," Alexis said as she hugged Ladon closer.

Ladon shook his head. "There was only one explosion. That's not an attack."

"Then what was that?" Ryuu asked.

"If Cadmus is to be believed…something much worse."

Ryuu opened his mouth to demand further explanation when a monstrous roar of dragon challenged echoed through the facility. The roar was so powerful that Alexis had to cover her ears. Everyone knew that the sheer size of the creature that produced such a sound must be massive.

Ladon kissed Alexis passionately and held her tightly in his arms, "No matter what happens please remember that I have never loved someone the way that I loved you. Gaia blessed me when she put you in my path."

"Why does it feel like you are saying goodbye," Alexis's voice cracked. Ladon was emotional ad his walls weren't up as strong as they normally were. She felt his resolve to face whatever it was that Cadmus had told him about and he planned on doing it alone so no one else would have to die.

"No," she whispered as tears gathered in her eyes. "No, you can't, Ladon."

Ladon looked down into Alexis's eyes and held her gaze. He then closed his eyes and laid his forehead against hers with a sigh. Once last caress of her cheek and he then pushed her into Tugarin's arms.

"Keep her safe," he said as Tugarin nodded.

Ladon then turned to walk out of the research facility. Alexis struggled against Tugarin's hold screaming for Ladon to stop and find another way. When Ladon disappeared from her sight she turned on Tugarin and beat his chest.

"Damn it! He plans on sacrificing himself. He believes that he is going to die!" Alexis screamed as pushed against the immovable blue dragon.

"He's doing what he must to keep you safe, Alexis." Tugarin shook her in anger but held her tenderly when she fell against him sobbing. "Honor his deep love for you and don't make this more difficult for him than it already is. He can feel you through your connection. Give him strength, not grief. Grief can come after if the worst happens."

Tugarin rubbed Alexis's back and stroked her hair until her cries subsided. He may have scolded her, but he understood. She and Ladon were bonded mates. Humans would call it a true love match. Many Drakonians had glorified the bonding to the point that they believed it to be some mystical power surge. But the real power was the lengths people were willing to go to for someone they truly loved.

Suddenly Alexis pushed away from Tugarin. His initial reaction was she was going to go after Ladon, but she took off in the opposite direction. It left him and Ryuu just standing in the hallway unsure of what to do next.

Ryuu sighed and gave Tugarin a slight grin. "Sometimes those two can make you feel right useless; can't they?"

Tugarin gave a gruff chuckle, "I suppose we should prove we aren't useless." He looked down the hall in the direction that Alexis disappeared to. "She's going to get information from Cadmus. We should gather information about what is outside and what weaponry is available."

"Her bedroom is down that direction as well. How can you be sure she is going to Cadmus? She maybe going to worry in private."

Tugarin leveled a look on Ryuu.

"Okay, you're right...Alexis wouldn't cry in private, she would try to find a solution."

Tugarin clapped Ryuu on his back, "You go see what the monitors are saying and I will figure out what we can use as weaponry. By the time we are done, Alexis should have her information."

The two men spent the next half hour gathering information and weapons. There weapon stores were minimal. This was a research facility and not a military outpost after all. Tugarin made note that They would need to begin fortifying their properties more as long as Fafnir remained a threat.

Ladon had sent one update about fifteen minutes ago stating that he had not found the enemy but there was a large amount of smoke rising in the distance and he was heading that direction. Ryuu confirmed that the sensors recorded that the whole ship had crashed. Which added another thing they would have to take care of, hopefully before the human authorities could get there.

Finally, Alexis returned from speaking with Cadmus. The grim look on her face told Tugarin that whatever she had been told wasn't a good thing. His supposition was confirmed when she described

what Ladon would be facing. Tugarin was certain
that given time he could figure out a way to take care
of the abomination that Fafnir had created. But one
thing they didn't have was time.

After hearing what Ryuu and Tugarin found,
Alexis came up with a plan. It was bold and might
get them all killed, but it was better than just sitting
there.

"Are you sure we should have left Cadmus in the control room?" Ryuu asked for the third time as they trudged through the snow towards the black smoke rising in the sky.

"He willing let me into his mind, Ryuu. He was as much a victim of Fafnir as you were." Alexis stumbled in a particularly deep snow bank. It was slow going without the sled and dogs. But the sled still needed to be repaired before it would be usable again.

As they got closer the air became more thick with smoke. Alexis was worried that when they found the remains of the ship that they would only find a burned-out husk. They needed to know if any of the remaining crew survived, especially Fafnir's Frankenstein.

Over the last ridge of snow, they found the smoldering remains of the Drakonian ship. It was actually much smaller than Alexis had assumed it would be, covering the area of a New York high rise if it was laid on the ground instead of in the air. She had assumed that a vessel meant for deep space travel would have needed the space of a city.

"Looks like a newer version of the military's rapid response vessels," Ryuu said as he crested the ridge of snow to look down on the ship below.

"Makes sense considering how quickly they got here from Drakos," Tugarin added. "Let's go see what we can find." He called as he was already sliding down the slope towards the ship.

The ship had cracked in two when it crashed. The front part taking the most damage. That was where the flames had been confined. Alexis and two walked around the rear of the vessel until they found the hatch. They reached out with their nano machines, only to discover that the ship was dead and wouldn't respond. They used and area that had been sheared away in the crash to crawl through to enter the ship. It was a fairly easy fit for Alexis but the two dragons struggled to squeeze through. When all three were in the ship they turned on the lights they had packed in from the research facility.

Alexis gasped at what she saw. The interior of the ship was a bloody mess, literally. Body parts flung hither and yon, blood splattered not only on the floor but the walls and ceiling as well.

"Did the crash do this?" Ryuu asked as he raised the light to get an idea of what lay further ahead.

"No. If the crash had killed them the bodies would still be mostly intact." Tugarin leaned down to look at a severed arm. "Whatever did this ripped the crew apart. I doubt they were alive when they crashed."

"The monster got loose." Alexis looked around at the carnage. "Maybe the creature died in the crash."

Tugarin stood up and pulled a laser rifle from its holster, "We can certainly hope."

"Let's see if we can locate a body. If we can,

then we can call Ladon back." Alexis carefully picked her way through the gore to head deeper into the ship.

They passed the mess hall and moved through the bodies they found near the recreation area. Nothing living stirred in the darkened ship. Alexis was beginning to feel like she was in a horror movie. With each turn in the path her heart jumped expecting the villain to jump out to slaughter them. But despite her mounting fear she trudged on. She had to find out if Ladon was still in danger. The need to protect him overrode any fear that she felt.

They were going through what appeared to be the sleeping quarters of the crew when a faint pounding sound could be heard. Ryuu put a finger to his lips signaling the others to be quiet. The two dragons naturally sandwiched Alexis between them for her protection. They followed the sound to a broken door at the end of the hall. Behind the door they could hear a faint voice calling for help.

Tugarin lifted his gun and nodded to Ryuu who wrenched the door open. They found a young Drakonian who was missing a couple of limbs, raising a weapon at them with a shaky arm. He had tried to stem the flow of blood by using wires from the ship to create tourniquets on the missing arm and leg, but he was still bleeding out. The effort to hold the gun was too much and it clattered to the ground as the young man dropped his remaining arm to the floor with a groan.

"Go ahead…kill me," the young crew member gasped between ragged breaths.

"We have to help him," Alexis cried as she rushed forward.

Tugarin pulled her back with a shake of his head.

"But we have to try, he's just a kid."

With a sigh, Tugarin handed Alexis his weapon and kneeled next to the young man. He already knew that the boy was dying because he had lost too much blood; but he sent his nanos out to diagnose and ease his pain.

The strain around the young Drakonian's eyes eased at Tugarin's touch and he closed his eyes with a sigh. Still blood poured from his wounds. Every passing second he became more pale and his breathing more raspy. Even Alexis could see that they weren't going to save him. Tears fell down her cheeks as she tried to rationalize that at least they were able to ease his pain.

Suddenly, a loud thump rocked the ship. The young crew member's eyes opened wide and the last thing he gasped before breathing his last was, "Run!"

*****

Ladon had scoured the area and saw no sign of the enemy. He saw the ship enter orbit and crash, but so far he could see any sign of anyone leaving the crash site. If they were lucky everyone would have perished in the crash. But Ladon's instincts were itching the back of his neck like being watched by a predator. The last time he had this feeling was in the middle of skirmish on Axion Prime. Listening had saved his life then and he is not about to dismiss his instincts this time around.

He took to the sky to cover more ground. He kept a sharp eye out for anyone moving away from the crash site. What he found was a small group trekking towards the crash site. Part of him wanted to rage at Alexis and the others. He had left them at the research facility to keep Alexis safe.

Ladon's dragon groaned. If Alexis decided that the course of action she should take was the right one, no one would be able to stop her. At least Ryuu and Tugarin were armed. He should be thankful for small things he supposed.

Ladon swooped in and out of the black smoke that filled the sky. He opened all of his dragon senses. Underneath the bitter smell of the burning shift there was the coppery tang of spilled blood…a lot of it. He lost sight of the trio as they found a way into the downed vessel.

Ladon landed and shifted into his humanoid form near the front of the ship. It was where the Drakos traditionally built the control center. It was engulfed in flames. Ladon sent out his nanos creating a bubble around him in which he could control the surrounding temperature. He climbed into the command center for the Drakonian ship. Inside he found the bodies of two of the bridge officers. The fire had desiccated their bodies to the point that no clues were left to what had happened.

Drakonian ships had several layers of safety protocols. It might end up floating dead in orbit, but it should have crashed to the Earth. There was nothing left to discover in the command center. They might be able to pull some information from the central computer if other parts of the ship were in better shape.

Ladon climbed through the debris and flames until he could muscle open the hatch that lead to the rest of the ship. It was around that area that the ship had split in two upon impact. The break had contained the flames to forward part of the ship. The rest had minor damage by comparison.

Ladon picked his way through the twisted metal. The further away he got from the flames the stronger the smell of blood became. When he got past the tear in the frame he slipped on something wet. Looking down he could see a dark pool surrounding the remains of a severed limb. Ladon called upon his dragon half to partially shift his eyes so he could see in the darkened interior. As far as he could see down the vessel's hall was body parts and blood. It looked like the set of a horror movie.

He looked down at the leg that was lying next to his foot. Ladon frowned, there was something odd about the limb. He picked up the leg so he could examine it. There was the torn tissue one would expect from a limb that had been ripped from the body. But there was also bruising around the ankle that looked like a large clawed hand. Upon closer examination dragon teeth marks surrounded areas of torn flesh.

Ladon frowned. Just what the hell had happened on this ship?

Ladon's instincts were screaming at him that the danger was still present and he needed to get to

Alexis. He tuned his nanos to their shared connection and started to move quickly through the carnage. The dead were the dead and nothing would bring them back. They could deal with funerary rites later. Ladon was more concerned with the state of the living.

He followed the pull of his nanos to track Alexis through the maze of the ship's interior. As he searched for her Ladon couldn't stop his mind from speculating about what happened on this ship. Every scenario he came up with turned his blood cold.

The closer he got to Alexis the more signs he saw that something besides them was alive on this ship; something that was eating the dead.

Ladon turned was last corner, Alexis was very close. He could feel it. He stopped when a loud thump rocked the ship. He crouched into a fighter's stance and slowed his forward movement. He pulled two retractable blades from his uniform pack. A projectile weapon might have given him the advantage of distance; but no one had ever been able to best him when it came to close quarters combat.

He crept up to the next bend in the hall. He could hear grunts and heavy breathing. He rounded the corner prepared to attack. What he saw froze the blood in his veins. A huge deformed monster stuck somewhere between dragon and man had his face buried in the bloody stomach of young soldier who couldn't have been long out of the educational system. Thankfully the blank eyes of the young man's body told Ladon that his spirit had already passed from this realm. Still the sight turned his stomach and Ladon wasn't able to completely suppress his gag as his stomach rebelled.

The creature slowly turned his fevered gazed to Ladon. His fanged mouth curling into a bloody smile.

"Warm meat…" it rasped as it stuffed the dead soldier's entrails into its maw of a mouth.

The creature slowly stood and Ladon understood just how large that thing really was. It nearly filled the spacious hall and had to stoop to prevent its head from hitting the ceiling. Ladon knew that he would not be able to maneuver in this space with something that big.

He turned and started looking for a way out into the open. Hopefully his dragon form could take on that creature.

The monster's roar filled the entire ship. If Ladon had been less of a warrior that bellow alone would have defeated him. This wasn't like any battle he had fought before. He had to find that thing's weakness fast or none of them may survive.

Alexis stopped when a roar shook the ship from where they had just come from.

"Ladon…"

She pushed her consciousness through the nanos that connected her and Ladon and Screamed when her vision faded and she was surrounded by what Ladon saw. The thing pursuing him was straight out of a nightmare. She felt that Ladon was trying to find a way out of the ship. She forced his eyes away from the creature and to look around.

I don't have time for you to take over my mind, Alexis. She heard Ladon growling in her mind and ignored him. He was near where they had entered, she recognized a particular piece of twisted metal that looked almost like a bow.

About three meters up ahead, there is a tear in the hull. It is difficult to see if you don't know it is there. That's where we came in. It will be a tight fit, but big and ugly won't be able to get through. She pushed the images of what she relayed into his mind.

Fine. Get out of my mind and get your ass back to the research facility.

Love you too, asshole.

She severed her connection to Ladon and turned without a word to the worried looking men following her. They had to get off this ship she wasn't going to stay around to be that things next meal.

The group made it to the rear hatch of the ship. This had been the cargo area. Crates and equipment were thrown everywhere. In one corner, they found a macabre shine created with the severed heads of the crew. The creature had stacked them like a pyramid on a crate next to an area that looked almost like a nest.

Alexis's stomach heaved and she turned away from Ryuu and Tugarin to empty what little had been contained within. It was one thing to the carnage of severed limbs and blood. It was an entirely different thing to see the faces of the victims frozen in screams of horror.

Tugarin rubbed her back as she wiped her mouth with the back of her hand.

"We need to get out of here. Are you able to continue?" Tugarin asked gently.

"Get us out of here." Almost as soon as the words passed Alexis lips she grabbed her head and cried out.

Help me…

An unfamiliar voice was invading her mind. It was faint buried underneath the clawing pain she recognized as Fafnir's control mechanism. But the pain wasn't directed at her. She knew that she should cut off the connection but something in the despair of the voice in her mind kept her from shutting it off.

Tugarin scooped up the incapacitated Alexis.

He nodded at Ryuu who used the large area of the cargo space to transform into his midnight dragon. Ryuu then used his great strength to rip the rear hatch open. He returned to his human form and the three rushed out into the soviet tundra.

They ducked behind what little scrub was in the area as a large shadow passed over them. Alexis looked up and saw the sparkling red dragon that was Ladon. A second shadow passed over them and the pleading voice got louder.

The second shadow was a monstrous creature that was more machine than dragon. It was easily twice the size of Ladon and was covered in undulating mass of nano machines. There were so many of them that they could be seen with the naked eye. The sheer mass of them made even Tugarin gasp.

"By the gods, what has that demented dragon done?" Tugarin lowered Alexis to the ground without taking his eyes off the creature trailing Ladon.

"Is that what I think it is?" Ryuu asked.

"No wonder that thing has gone mad. With that many nanos he must be in tremendous amounts of pain…they would have to be using his own body for energy and raw material."

"It's not the pain that is driving him mad," Alexis commented while rubbing her temples. "It is being trapped within your own body, seeing all the horrors first hand and not being able to do anything about it. Not even being able to die to stop the horror of your life."

"You connected to that thing?" Tugarin glared at her. She knew he was angry because he was afraid of her being in danger.

"I didn't do it on purpose," Alexis sighed.

Before Tugarin could lecture her, the creature caught up with Ladon. Ladon's dragon shifted in the air to face his enemy with a massive battle roar. The creature answered him in kind.

Ladon tucked his wings and shot towards the monster. As he closed he distance, Ladon extended his claws to shred the underbelly of the beast. He was quicker and more maneuverable than the massive monster. He scored a solid hit and blood rained down on the snow, staining flowers of battle in the pristine white landscape.

Ryuu whooped because that kind of blow should down a dragon. But it quickly became clear that he had celebrated too soon. The moving mass of nanos quickly converged on the wounds repairing them midair at a speed that shocked the other dragons.

Ladon circled and dived shredding the creature with claws and burning him with flame. The thing roared in rage with each hit. The nanos kept the creature from going down. But Alexis watched the battle closely. She knew like the others that Ladon could keep up his attacks for only so long. She was so intent on the battle that she was the only one to notice that Fafnir's experiment was learning from each attack.

The creature's movements were less clumsy. Its movement was beginning to match Ladon's. The nanos that controlled the creature were copying the moves of its opponent. No wonder Cadmus was so certain that this thing was certain death.

Alexis couldn't swallow the cry of horror as the monster crashed into Ladon, latching on with claws and enveloping him with its wings. The creature looked directly at her with a snarl.

Please, help me.

She rubbed her temple as the pain washed through her.

Let Ladon go and we will help you. She was fairly certain that the voice in her head was the mind of whoever had been used to create the thing now battling Ladon.

I can't... The voice wailed in despair.

"Look!" Ryuu pointed to the sky. Ladon and the monster grappled. Blood from both rained down. Ladon reached up to shred the creature's wings. As the nano machines rushed to heal the wounds of Fafnir's abomination they continued swarming towards Ladon.

His right claw was covered with the tiny machines up to his elbow when Ladon bellowed in pain. Alexis opened her connection to him and flooded him with strength. She could feel the invading nanos attempting to assimilate Ladon into raw material.

Break away! She cried in his mind.

Ladon wrenched his claw away from the creature, but the multitude of nanos already attached to his body began restricting his movement. He could no longer keep his wings open to fly. He crashed into the snow.

Alexis took off running towards Ladon.

Don't come any closer! Ladon snarled in her mind.

I can't just leave you, she cried.

Yes, you can. Get as far away from here as possible.

Alexis could feel Ladon's resolve in her mind. He knew he was facing death. He was afraid of what would happen once the enemy nanos fully integrated him. But regardless of his fate he knew that if any of the others got within reach that they would suffer the same fate.

She could feel his energy draining as he fought to keep the nanos out of his mind while his brain planned and discarded scenario after battle scenario. Ladon quickly concluded that an offensive attack while trying to defend his life wouldn't work. Alexis felt his resignation sigh through her entire body even as her mind screamed its denial. Ladon was going to attempt one last kamikaze attack. If he could take out the creature's heart and brain stem at the same time, it might prove to be enough damage that even the mutant nano machines wouldn't be able to recover from.

Alexis could feel something stirring within her; but she didn't have the time to examine what it was. She knew that if Ladon went through with his plan he would die. She also knew that at the rate the enemy nanos were multiplying Ladon would never live to complete his suicide mission.

She knew that once he made up his mind that she couldn't stop Ladon. But, Alexis had to do something. *Think, Alexis. This is just another puzzle to solve,* she told herself. The men had told her that every Drakonian had an affinity to control something. She was now Drakonian. What could she control? She had tried playing with fire and water like Ladon and Ryuu, but that hadn't worked. She couldn't diagnose illness like Tugarin. But all three told her that her nano machines were unusually powerful. Why? She started rapidly replaying the times that she used her nanos in her mind.

Then it clicked. Her nanos talent was taking over other nanos. It was how she kept Fafnir from controlling her nanos. It was how she easily invaded the minds of those around her. She could send strength to anyone she chose. But she needed to do more than send strength this time. She had to completely shut down the enemies nanos invading Ladon.

Could she do it? There was only one way to find out.

Tugarin elbowed Ryuu and pointed at Alexis. She was visibly shaking and tears tracked down her cheeks as she stared intently at Ladon. The two dragons could feel the buzz of their communications because of the abnormal strength of Alexis's nano machines. But what made both dragons step back in surprise was the rippling of pale white scales tipped in blue and black across her skin. She was like a young dragon trying to shift for the first time. But even full blooded Drakonian females couldn't shift.

"How is that even possible?" Tugarin asked Ryuu.

"I don't know," Ryuu whispered.

Tugarin heard a strange note in Ryuu's voice and turned to look directly at the black dragon. "But you have an idea, don't you?"

Ryuu shook his head. "I thought it was just a tick of the light when she almost died of the mating bite fever. The scales didn't actually emerge like they are doing now, but during the height of her fever I thought I saw something that looked like scale under her skin." He ran an agitated hand through his hair. "I looked through as much of the library as I could, but the only reference I ever came across was the story of an ancient human mate that shifted when her mate was in danger. It was written like a fairy tale…. a myth."

Tugarin looked back at Alexis. "Not so much of a myth anymore."

A large shadow crossed overhead and the two men flinched. They had gotten distracted by Alexis and almost forgot about the monstrous enemy circling overhead.

"We need to get to cover." Ryuu headed

towards Alexis.

Suddenly Ladon launched himself into the air as Alexis screamed. She turned to the other men.

"Help him! He plans on sacrificing himself."

Ryuu looked up to where Ladon was winging his way towards the creature. He frowned, something was different.

"Where are the nano machines that were covering him?"

"I shut them down," Alexis slashed her hand through the air. "Does it really matter? He's going to die without help and that thing is going to continue to wreak havoc across this world."

Tugarin sighed. "She's got a point. We need to stop this thing here."

Ryuu shifted and took to the air. His black form a sharp contrast of the bright tundra. Tugarin hugged Alexis and whispered for her to be safe before his blue joined the colors in the sky.

Ryuu knocked Ladon off course; keeping him from his suicide attack. Alexis expanded her mind to hear all three dragons. Ladon was equal parts angry and relieved at his attack being thwarted.

Deep down he still wanted to grow old with Alexis.

She heard Ladon explain his logic about destroying the heart and brain stem to keep the nano machines from saving the creature from death. The three organized their attack.

Ladon attacked head on, distracting the creature while the other dragons circled around. But Fafnir's Frankenstein wasn't so easy to out maneuver. He refused to fall into the trap the three dragons set.

Help me!

The pain clawed through Alexis's head and rippled through her entire body. She could feel that the being trapped within the body of the monster no longer had any control at all. His clumsy movements at the beginning of the fight were equal parts the nanos learning from its opponents and the organic being fighting for control.

The creature remained on the defensive for a while; but just like with Ladon its nano machines soon learned the patterns that the three dragons fought in. Soon it turned to offensive attacks.

The first one it took out was Tugarin. It grabbed the blue dragon as he circled close to attempt to take out the creature from behind. It moved so fast that Alexis missed the hit that shattered Tugarin's wing; but she saw the aftermath as Tugarin tumbled to the ground, one wing flapping uselessly in the air as the other struggled to control his descent. He hit the snow and ice with a sickening crunch.

Alexis actually laughed in relief when his cursing and intense pain swept over her. At least he was alive.

Can you deactivate these damn things? Tugarin called to Alexis.

She sent instructions for the frequency that shut down the creature's nanos to Tugarin. The first wave they encountered deactivated quickly. The second wave not so much.

"Damn they are adapting like the freaking Borg," Alexis said through clenched teeth. She hoped that *Star Trek's* solution worked here. She cycled through similar but slightly different frequencies until she hit on another one to shut down the nano machines.

In the short time, it took her to deal with Tugarin's nano problem, both Ryuu and Ladon had engaged the beast. They wrapped around the creature ripping and tearing with claws and teeth. The creature's nano machines had swarmed across all of them. It was impossible to tell where the creature ended and the other dragons began. The nanos restricted Ladon and Ryuu's movement which in turn restricted the creatures.

Soon the three appeared to just be an undulating metallic mass suspended in midair. At least until they started falling.

"NO!"

Alexis scrambled towards the area where they fell. She could feel both dragons being devoured by the nano machines. She could hear the individual trapped within the creature weeping in pain and despair.

She could feel Ladon dying.

It couldn't end this way. It just couldn't. She had just recently realized that she loved him. He was the only one she could believe loved her without question forever. She couldn't lose him. She couldn't go back to those days devoid of love and filled with doubt about her own worth. Ladon gave her love and showed her own self-worth.

She had no idea what she could do to save

him. But she ran anyway because she had to do something. As she ran she didn't notice that she began to move faster. She ignored the itch beneath her skin. Then the beast rose from the mass of living nanos and raised its head to the sky to roar its triumph.

Alexis put on a burst of speed without realizing that her body was changing. Her legs elongated and became more muscular. She stretched clawed hands forward as wings burst from her back. Her face elongated as fangs erupted in her mouth. Scales rippled down her body until the human Alexis was no more and a beautiful dragon took flight in her place.

The dragon Alexis knew that she couldn't defeat the creature by size. She was delicate in comparison. But she was fast. And the strength of her nanos was on par with the creatures. The difference being she had full control of hers.

She hit the creature square in the chest throwing the thing off balance and preventing the fatal strike of its claws at the injured Ladon. Instead the creature's claws sunk into her back, but she ignored the pain. She called on all her strength and poured it into her nanos. She intuitively used the virus that was within her body to infect and reprogram the creatures nanos until the first wave turned on the next.

The monster convulsed beneath her as her dragon pinned it to the ground. It was the control of the nanos that made her capable of such a feat outside of what her body was capable of performing. With each wave of nanos converted her strength grew. She removed the commands that forced the machines to continuously seek out new raw material, halting their reproduction.

As the wave of nano machines turned in her favor the creature ceased to struggle. It raised its giant clawed hand and gently caressed Alexis's face. She screamed as a lifetime of information flooded into her mind. The man Fafnir had experimented on to create this monster wanted her to have as much information as possible. It was flashing through her mind so fast that she knew it would take months for her to sort through it all.

Thank you…

The words whispered though her mind as the images faded and the creature breathed its last. The body that had artificially been kept alive and together fell apart. Without a consciousness to hold them together, the remaining multitude of nano machines swirled around Alexis as her dragon stood

372

and roared to the sky.

She turned and walked back towards Ladon and Ryuu, shifting back to her human form as she went. Tugarin watched in awe as the cloud of nanos formed around her. Energy arched through the cloud in a multitude of colors as the nanos swirled and followed her. She was a goddess on Earth in that moment. She was Kali and Kali Ma all in one…creation and destruction both. For a moment, even Tugarin was afraid of her.

48

Alexis could feel the added power of the nano machines that swarmed around her. Having control of so many gave her unbridled strength. It also allowed her mind to process at a much faster rate as the nanos took on part of the processes of her synapses. She quickly catalogued the things she would be able accomplish. Fafnir was insane, but the old dragon was still a genius. If he had actually cared about the people he used, he could have conquered the universe.

Despite the near addictive rush that the power of the nanos gave her she knew that she wouldn't be able to sustain this for long. These new nanos required a constant influx of energy and raw material. Between that and Fafnir's demented control it was no wonder that the poor man who had been the original creature had been nearly driven mad with pain and despair. It was a testament of his strength that he still fought Fafnir's control.

Alexis heard Ladon's cry of pain more than felt it. The swarm of nanos was overloading her senses. They were still being devoured by nanos under Fafnir's control. Alexis turned and walked towards them, concentrating on her connection to the two dragons to guide her more than her sight which was obscured by the cloud of nano machines surrounding her.

She nearly tripped over Ryuu. She knew that Ladon had fallen near Ryuu. She concentrated and the nanos parted like the red sea so she could see once again. She kneeled between the two men. Ryuu had lost consciousness; but Ladon was watching her with pain filled eyes. He clenched his teeth as another wave of nanos destroyed bits of him.

Alexis kneeled between the two men and laid a hand on each. The nanos swarming around her

375

swirled down her arm to cover the men. The machines started reporting back the injuries of the men as they infected the enemy nanos with the virus to sever their connection with Fafnir. Soon the nanos were inert awaiting orders from Alexis.

The damage to the two men was extensive. The nanos had consumed a large amount of their body; to the point of even damaging major organ systems. Alexis knew that Ladon was still conscious by sheer strength of will alone.

"You are really hurt, my love," Alexis said as she laid her forehead against his. Ladon's eyes softened for a moment before another wave of pain wracked his system. "I think I can fix it, but it's going to hut like hell."

Ladon reached a shaky hand up to caress he cheek before wincing in pain. "Just do it." He laid back, closing his eyes. His breathing was ragged.

Without a second thought Alexis reactivated the inert nanos and added part of the multitude that flew around her until both men disappeared from sight. She connected to Tugarin, startling the man.

I need your medical expertise to help repair the damage to Ladon and Ryuu.

What do you need me to do?

Can you see through me to the nanos?

Not really.

Damn...I need to tell them what to repair.

Tugarin smiled slightly. In a way, it reassured him that Alexis didn't know everything after her god-like appearance earlier.

The nanos should know Drakonian anatomy. Did you wipe their memory banks?

No, I just severed their connection to Fafnir and then coopted them.

Then they should know what Ladon and Ryuu started with before they began taking them apart. Just instruct them to return Ladon and Ryuu to their original forms and then use their repair functions to deal with any injuries that deviate from standard Drakonian anatomy.

Alexis rolled her eyes. *You make it sound so easy.*

She heard Tugarin laugh but she turned her concentration to the cloud of nano machines that currently covered the man she loved and her dear

377

friend. She sent out the instructions and waited.

For a moment, she worried that it hadn't worked because she couldn't see that anything was happening. Then Ryuu's body convulsed and Ladon cried out. The nanos started moving. It looked almost as if the men had been covered in swarming insects. It was a bit nauseating but Alexis refused to turn away.

Ladon's body jerked and he started screaming. He just kept screaming until his voice was hoarse. Alexis wondered what the hell she had done to him. She was about to stop the whole process when suddenly everything stopped and there was silence.

The nanos retreated to swarm once more around Alexis. They revealed a very pale, very still Ladon. Alexis was terrified that she had killed him and a scream welled up in her mind.

Alexis jumped when a hand landed on her shoulder.

"He's just unconscious, my dear," Tugarin said as he waved a hand in front of his face to chase away the nanos. "Could you do something about these things?"

Alexis took a deep breath and called the nanos to her. They coalesced into an intricate suit of armor.

Tugarin whistled, "That's a neat little trick." He looked around the barren landscape. They were a good distance away from the research facility and the two sleeping dragons weren't going to get there under their own steam. His nanos were telling him that the multitude of nanos that Alexis now controlled were already taxing her system. It would be dangerous to ask her to use them to transport Ladon and Ryuu with her new nanos.

He took out the small communicator that he brought with them and examined it. Amazingly it had made it through the battle relatively undamaged. He sent a few of his own nanos into the communicator to switch it on.

"…What the hell is happening? Is Anyone out there? The sensors are going crazy. Are you dead?" Tugarin winced and adjusted the volume.

"We're fine, Cadmus." He replied.

"Thank Gaia you are still alive." Cadmus sighed over the comm. "How many did we lose? And do I need to start setting the traps?"

"When I said 'we're fine' I meant all of us."

"All?"

"Yes."

"How?"

"It's a long story, Cadmus. We will fill you in once we get back. Do you think you are strong enough to bring out one of the gravitational load sleds?"

"Yeah, I think so. Do I need to bring extra weapons?"

Tugarin laughed as he looked over at Alexis and his friends. She was brushing the hair from Ladon's face and still checking him over to make sure that the nanos didn't miss anything. "No, Cadmus. The threat has been neutralized. But a cargo stasis box might be a good idea."

Tugarin turned off the communicator before the former captive soldier started interrogating him on how they killed off one of Fafnir's most feared creatures. He sank into the snow and flopped on his back. The aurora seemed particularly bright this evening. It really was a beautiful sight. Zoya used to love to watch the lights in the sky.

His heart seized a little at the thought of his beloved Zoya. He turned his head to watch Alexis, his only living relative (at least as far as he knew). He could hear Zoya in his mind telling him that Alexis needed him and he knew it was true. The battle with Fafnir was far from over. And as petty as it may be, Tugarin wanted to live until he knew Fafnir was dead. While he loved Alexis like a daughter, it would be the thought of revenge that kept him in this world.

"Tugarin," Alexis called.

He pushed up from the snow and shook his head as he stood. Plans could be made later.

Ladon woke up to Alexis's face.

"I must have died because I see an angel."

Alexis promptly punched him in the chest before kissing him senseless. "I almost lost you." Ladon could feel tears dropping onto his face.

"Hey, we're here and we're okay." Ladon reached up and cupped her face. He looked around. "Where's your cloud?"

Alexis looked confused for a minute then she remembered. "Oh, the nanos? Tugarin helped me put them into stasis. I suggested disassembling them, but he seemed convinced that we would need them again sometime."

Ladon struggled into a sitting position. Damn, he was weak. "He's probably right. How long was I out?"

Alexis looked at the monitors, "A little over a day. Tugarin says you will need to take it easy since a huge amount of your body is freshly repaired and needs time to fully heal. He wants you to stay in bed for a while."

"Well I know a few ways you could keep me in bed," Ladon waggled his eyebrows at her and Alexis laughed.

"You and I both know that does not constitute rest."

"I promise I will just lay here and let you do all of the work."

Alexis leaned over and whispered something into Ladon's ear. His eyes widened and his mouth hung open.

"...But you only get that if you rest and fully

383

recover."

Ladon snapped a salute, "Yes, ma'am." He leaned back his strength suddenly sapped. "Did Ryuu make it?"

Alexis sighed, "It was touch and go for a little while. The nanos had gotten to his nervous system by the time I got to him. We repaired it, but his body had to retrain his new nerves. Tugarin set up a physical therapy area for him down the hall. Hopefully in a few weeks both of you will be as good as new."

Cadmus entered with a tray of water and some snacks. Ladon realized just how hungry he was.

"Thanks, Cadmus," Alexis said as the man nodded and left the room. She turned back to Ladon, "He still doesn't talk much but he has been a tremendous help."

Ladon looked at the door thoughtfully, "There are going to be a lot more like him." Ladon heaved a big sigh. "If this was the past I would say that Earth would be an excellent asylum; but humanity doesn't know about dragons and you have developed to a point that the sudden discovery that you are not alone in the world could have devastating consequences for the planet. Humans have grown into a rather reactionary species."

Alexis handed Ladon a small sandwich which he promptly swallowed.

"Woman, you realize as a dragon I need more food than this," Ladon said right before his sandwich tried to make a second appearance.

"You were saying?"

Ladon chose to ignore her smug look. "We need a solid plan, which includes not only places to put the Drakonians we will end up collect but also an offensive and defensive strategy."

Alexis raised an imperious brow at Ladon.

"You and Tugarin have already started coming up with plans, haven't you? What are you going to need from me?"

"Your money mostly. Unfortunately, we are probably going to need a bit more than you currently have."

Ladon laughed, "And here I thought you loved me for my looks."

Alexis leaned over and kissed Ladon deeply.

She laid her forehead against his, a gesture that had come to mean love and comfort to both of them, and sighed. "I love you for a lot of reasons, Ladon Drake. You and me to the ends of time."

Ladon wrapped his arms around his mate, "Until the ends of time."

Ryuu pounded on the condo door.

"Damn it, Ladon. We're late!"

"Just go on without us," came the muffled reply followed by a feminine giggle.

"You're the fucking bride and groom. I can't go on without you."

"We'll be out shortly," Alexis called as Ryuu left the door in a huff.

Ladon rolled over and pinned Alexis to the

bed as she tried to get up. "You would think this was his wedding the way he is acting."

Alexis laughed and kissed Ladon's nose. "Well he did do most of the planning, so it kind of is his wedding."

Ladon captured her lips and nipped and suckled. His kisses moved down her neck and across her chest.

"Ladon, we are going to be late."

"So?" His tongue circled her nipple. "It's not like they can start without us."

"But it's rude to keep our guests waiting," Alexis gasped as he sucked her nipple into his mouth.

His hands moved lower until his fingers buried into her dampening entrance.

Alexis wrapped her legs around Ladon and rolled until he was pinned beneath her. It was at this moment that a grinning Ladon decided to try and get out of bed.

"We can't keep our guests waiting, love."

Alexis narrowed her eyes at him and grabbed

his hips as he playfully tried to dodge her. She kissed him across his stomach as he continued to stammer that they needed to get going. When she slipped his hardened manhood into her mouth he hissed.

"Fuck it! They can wait."

Ladon threw Alexis back on the bed as she giggled.

By Gaia, he loved this woman.

ABOUT THE AUTHOR

B.D. Snowden is a Texas native living in the Great Plains with her children of both two-legged and four-legged varieties. She is a voracious reader whose book habit literally brought a small town library to life. One day, when she was unable to get something new to read, she started turning the stories floating through her head into concrete concepts on paper. Find information about new releases and appearances at:
Geekygothblog.wordpress.com
Facebook.com/BrandiceSnowdenWriter